FRAMED!

JAMES PONTI

ALADDIN
New York London Toronto Sydney New Delhi

This book is a work of fiction. Any references to historical events, real people, or real places are used fictitiously. Other names, characters, places, and events are products of the author's imagination, and any resemblance to actual events or places or persons, living or dead, is entirely coincidental.

ALADDIN
An imprint of Simon & Schuster Children's Publishing Division
1230 Avenue of the Americas, New York, New York 10020
First Aladdin paperback edition May 2017
Text copyright © 2016 by James Ponti
Cover illustration copyright © 2016 by Paul Hoppe
Also available in an Aladdin hardcover edition.
All rights reserved, including the right of reproduction in whole or in part in any form.
ALADDIN is a trademark of Simon & Schuster, Inc., and related logo is
a registered trademark of Simon & Schuster, Inc.
For information about special discounts for bulk purchases, please contact Simon & Schuster
Special Sales at 1-866-506-1949 or business@simonandschuster.com.
The Simon & Schuster Speakers Bureau can bring authors to your live event.
For more information or to book an event contact the Simon & Schuster Speakers Bureau
at 1-866-248-3049 or visit our website at www.simonspeakers.com.
Cover designed by Laura Lyn DiSiena
Interior designed by Laura Lyn DiSiena and Steve Scott
The text of this book was set in Jansen.
Manufactured in the United States of America 1019 OFF
10 9
The Library of Congress has cataloged the hardcover edition as follows:
Names: Ponti, James, author.
Title: Framed! / by James Ponti.
Description: First Aladdin hardcover edition. | New York : Aladdin, 2016. |
Summary: In Washington, D.C., twelve-year-old Florian Bates, a consulting detective for the
FBI, and his best friend, Margaret, help thwart the biggest art heist in United States history.
Identifiers: LCCN 2015045506 (print) | LCCN 2016023737 (eBook) |
ISBN 9781481436304 (hardcover) | ISBN 9781481436328 (eBook)
Subjects: | CYAC: Mystery and detective stories. | United States. Federal Bureau of
Investigation—Fiction. | Friendship—Fiction. | Art thefts—Fiction. | Washington (D.C.)—
Fiction. | BISAC: JUVENILE FICTION / Mysteries & Detective Stories. | JUVENILE
FICTION / Action & Adventure / General. | JUVENILE FICTION / Humorous Stories.
Classification: LCC PZ7.P7726 Fr 2016 (print) | LCC PZ7.P7726 (eBook) | DDC [Fic]—dc23
LC record available at https://lccn.loc.gov/2015045506
ISBN 9781481436311 (pbk)

For Alex

1.

The (Not So) Safeway

MY NAME'S FLORIAN BATES. I'M TWELVE YEARS old and a seventh grader at Alice Deal Middle School in Washington, DC. My two favorite foods are pizza and egg rolls. I'm on the student council, I'm in the Scrabble club, and I plan to try out for soccer.

I also work for the FBI.

I know. That last one kind of comes out of the blue, doesn't it?

Technically they classify me as a "covert asset," which sounds very James Bond spylike but only means they want to keep me a secret. After all, it would be pretty embarrassing for them to admit they get help from a twelve-year-old, and it would be even worse if one of the guys on the Ten Most Wanted list showed up at my front door in a bad mood. So the covert part is good for both of us.

Becoming a detective wasn't something I meant to do. It just sort of happened because I notice things other people don't. My brain's weird that way. It spots details that seem insignificant and snaps them together like puzzle pieces.

The only people outside the Bureau who are supposed to know my status are my parents and my best friend Margaret. But that changed the day the Romanian Mafia kidnapped me after school. I was taking a shortcut behind the Safeway supermarket, and unless they were trying to influence any upcoming student council votes, it meant my identity was no longer a secret.

It's funny because earlier that day Margaret had warned me not to take that route. Normally we walk home together. But on Thursdays she has piano, so I go alone. That's when I look for shortcuts. Not because I'm in a hurry, but because it's like another puzzle.

"There are a lot of Dumpsters back there," she pointed out when I told her about it. "And you know what Ben Franklin said about Dumpsters. 'Nothing good ever happens when you're surrounded by them.'"

"I'm pretty sure Ben Franklin was dead about a hundred and fifty years before the Dumpster was invented," I countered.

"Then maybe I saw it on a poster. Either way, it's good advice. You shouldn't go back there."

"It may smell bad," I said, feeling suddenly defensive, "but it's not like it's dangerous or anything."

"Hmmm," she replied. "And how do you know that?"

I thought about it for a moment and smiled. "Because it's called the Safeway. If it was dangerous it would be called the Un-Safe Way."

She didn't find this nearly as clever as I did. So while I laughed, she just shook her head and said, "Boys are *soooo* funny." Then she leaned in close and added, "And *soooo* stupid."

Considering I was kidnapped in the exact place she warned me not to go, I'd say that little nugget belongs on a poster too. In my defense, I was going to walk the long way, but it started raining and I didn't want to get soaked.

I'd just squeezed through the gap in the fence and was hurrying behind the store holding my backpack over my head when I noticed the delivery truck. It should've been parked by the loading dock, but I was too busy worrying about getting wet to pay attention to that.

The rain was so hard I could see through its windshield only when the wipers swished across the glass. That's why

I didn't notice the driver had gotten out and left the engine running. I figured someone was just sitting inside waiting for the storm to pass.

When he stepped out from behind a Dumpster I almost crashed into him, which would have hurt because he was enormous. The sign on the truck said it belonged to a flower shop called the Happy Leprechaun, but this guy was neither. He was about six foot four, three hundred pounds, and looked like a professional wrestler. One of the villains.

He just stared at me, unconcerned about the rain pelting down on his giant bald scalp, and smiled. For a nanosecond I thought I was letting my imagination run wild. Then I looked down and noticed he wasn't wearing comfortable shoes like a delivery person would. He had on steel-toed work boots popular among factory workers, bricklayers, and international assassins.

I sprinted in the opposite direction, digging around in my backpack as I ran. I was trying to find the "panic button" the FBI had issued me. All I needed to do was push it twice and a team of agents would be put on instant alert. Unfortunately, he got to me before I got to it.

He tackled me and we skidded across the wet pavement into a pile of old fruit cartons. At first I thought I'd sliced my knee open, but what looked like blood turned out to be rotted strawberries smushed into my jeans. I tried to scramble up onto my feet, but he wrapped his arms around my head and put me in a sleeper hold. Just before I blacked out I looked at all the Dumpsters and told myself that I really should start following Margaret's advice.

I don't know how long I was unconscious, but when I woke up, I had a throbbing headache and was lying on the floor of the truck with my feet bound together and my hands tied behind my back.

I let out a low, painful moan. "Uunnnnnffff."

"Feel better if sleep," he said with a thick accent. "Twenty minute."

For a few seconds my vision was blurry, but when things came into focus I saw something beautiful—my backpack. He must have picked it up so no one would find it and come looking for me. That meant I still had a chance to press the panic button. I just needed to distract him long enough to scoot over to it.

I'd taken a hostage survival course at Quantico, the FBI training center, but at the time I couldn't imagine anyone wanting to kidnap me, so I didn't pay as much attention as I should have. Crazy stupid, I know, but at least I remembered the basics.

SURVIVAL STEP 1—Build a Rapport
with Your Captor

"That was an impressive tackle," I said. "Are you a football player?"

"Football is baby sport," he scoffed. "Pads. Helmets. I play man sport. Rugby."

"Well, I bet you're great at it," I said. "Did you play back home in Romania?"

He looked into the rearview mirror and eyed me suspiciously. "How you know I Romanian?"

I didn't want to tell him that the FBI had warned me that the Romanians were after me or that I saw the Romanian flag tattooed on his forearm when he put me in the sleeper hold. I wanted him to like me, so I tried buttering him up.

"My grandfather is from Romania," I said. "I have a picture of him when he was a soldier and he looks just like you."

This made him smile. (For the record my papa Gio is from Italy, and my grandpa Ted grew up in New Hampshire. But I think it's okay to lie when you've been abducted.)

"By the way, as one Romanian to another," I continued, "I think you've made a mistake. I think you nabbed the wrong kid."

The smile turned into a scowl and I worried that I'd offended him.

"I'm not saying you're not good at your job," I added. "It's just that with peer pressure and our need to fit in, kids look and dress so much alike that even we have trouble telling each other apart. One time my parents drove right by me at pickup. My own parents. So there's no shame in grabbing the wrong one."

"Not wrong," he replied forcefully.

SURVIVAL STEP 2—Disrupt Your Captor's Train of Thought

"Do you mean 'not wrong' as in *I'm* not wrong in what I'm saying? Or 'not wrong' as in *you're* not wrong in whom you kidnapped?"

I waited for a response, but all I heard was a low, frustrated growl. I assumed this was his deep-thinking noise.

"If you don't use pronouns, it really makes the conversation hard to follow. You need to say '*You're* not wrong' or '*I'm* not wrong.' Especially in a situation like this with threats and demands. The wrong pronoun could have someone else ending up with your ransom money, and that wouldn't be good for either one of us."

"Not wrong!" he barked again as if saying it louder suddenly solved the grammar issues. Just then he swerved to avoid another car, blasted his horn, and yelled what I assumed were choice Romanian curse words. I figured he was distracted enough for me to start inching toward my backpack.

"Don't feel bad," I continued. "I understand how hard it is to learn a new language. My family moves all the time. I've had to learn French and Italian. It's *molto difficile*. That's Italian for 'very difficult.'"

"Stop talk!"

"That's a perfect example of what I mean. You said 'stop talk' but it should be 'stop talking.' English is so complicated. But let's forget about grammar and get back to you kidnapping the wrong person. Like I said, it's an easy mistake and easy to fix. If you let me go, I promise not to tell anyone. Just drop me off at the nearest Metro station."

"Shut mouth or else!"

The "or else" was ominous, and combined with the continued lack of pronouns it reminded me of the third step from my training.

SURVIVAL STEP 3—Do Not Antagonize Your Captor

(When I told Margaret about the steps, she couldn't believe this wasn't first.)

So far I'd managed to get about halfway to the backpack, but I still needed one big push to reach it. When my FBI handler warned me about the Romanians, I did some studying and came across a website with phrases in different languages. I'd learned one just in case a moment like this arrived.

"Vehicolul meu aerian e plin cu maimute!"

I wasn't sure about my pronunciation, but it must have sounded Romanian enough because moments later he veered over to the side of the road and slammed on the brakes. The truck came to a screeching halt that sent me tumbling across the floor.

At this point the backpack was just beyond my fingertips. I was about to scoot the last little bit when he stood up, walked into the back of the delivery truck, and leaned over me, no regard for personal space (or dental hygiene).

"What saying you?" he demanded, his face red and splotchy.

"I said that if you let me go I won't tell anyone."

"No," he replied as he leaned even closer. "What saying you Romanian?"

I gulped and gave it another try, hoping I'd remembered it correctly. One wrong word could give the sentence a totally different meaning.

"Vehicolul meu aerian e plin cu maimute!"

Judging by his glower, I was pretty sure I'd ruined everything. I could just imagine the funeral, with my FBI instructor saying, "I told him not to antagonize his captor." And Margaret shaking her head and responding, "And I told him not to go behind the Safeway."

He reached down and pressed his beefy hands against the sides of my head, and I waited for the inevitable crushing of my skull. But that's not what happened. Instead he flashed a huge yellow-toothed grin and laughed.

"Hubbercraft?" he asked, mispronouncing the word as he continued to laugh.

"Yes," I replied, smiling back and repeating the phrase in English. "My hovercraft is full of monkeys." It was a silly phrase from a silly website, but it seemed to do the trick.

Rapport had finally been established.

"You're funny," he said as he helped me back into an upright position.

"Thanks," I replied. "By the way, 'You're funny' is excellent subject/verb agreement. I wonder if the fact that you were more relaxed helped . . ."

"Now shut mouth!"

Okay, so it was only limited rapport.

"Oh, and forget about backpack," he said. "I already took out what you're looking for."

He cackled and my heart sank.

"No call home for you," he added as he pulled my phone out of his shirt pocket and dangled it in the air. I tried not to show relief that he had only found my phone and not the panic button.

"Okay," I said, sounding as disappointed as I could. "No call home."

Fifteen minutes later we pulled off the highway onto a farm road and parked behind a barn. Everything was quiet for a moment until he said, "Do not joke when here. Understand?"

It was more of a warning than an order, as if the next person I met might not have a sense of humor.

"I understand," I replied. "Thank you."

He untied my feet and led me into the barn, my sneakers squishing down into the mud as we walked.

"Sit here and wait quiet," he instructed when we reached an old wooden picnic table.

SURVIVAL STEP 4—Brains Are Better Than Muscles

I knew I was about to come face-to-face with Nicolae Nevrescu, a ruthless gangster known as "Nic the Knife." He was the prime suspect in the case I was working on, and considering his reputation, I figured I was running out of time to act. The more I thought about my situation, the more upset it made me. And the more upset I got, the harder it was to breathe.

At first my breaths were slow and labored, but then I started to gasp for air.

"Quiet!" the kidnapper told me.

My gasping intensified and I leaned forward against the table in full panic mode.

"What is wrong?" he said.

I was trying to figure out how to hyperventilate and talk at the same time when a new voice came to my rescue.

"He needs his inhaler—*inhalator*," he said, using the Romanian word.

I looked up from the table and saw that it was Nevrescu.

"Yes," I wheezed as I nodded.

"Where it is?" asked the kidnapper.

"Back . . . pack," I gasped.

"Get it now!" said Nevrescu. "We can't let him die. At least not yet."

The massive man rushed back to the truck and grabbed my backpack. Since my hands were still tied behind my back he just dumped everything onto the table and I pointed at the inhaler with my head.

"Squeeze," I gasped.

He held it up to my mouth and pressed down while I sucked in a lungful of mist.

"Again," I said, my voice returning to somewhat normal.

He squeezed a second time and I sucked down some more mist.

You've got to hand it to the FBI. It looked and worked just like an actual inhaler. You'd never guess it was really a panic button.

"Thank you," I said with a huge sigh of relief. "You just saved my life."

Help was on the way. Now I only had to drag things out until it arrived.

Nevrescu sat down across the table from me and started to look through the papers strewn across the table. I don't know what ruthless crime lords are supposed to look like, but he looked more businesslike than I expected. His hair was cut stylishly, short on the sides, but a little thicker on top. He had a neatly trimmed beard and mustache and intense blue eyes. He also spoke with an accent, but his English was perfect.

"Florian Bates," he said, reading my name off the top of some homework. "You are the one the FBI only talks about in whispers. The one they call Little Sherlock."

"I have no idea what you're talking about," I said.

He gave me a disappointed look. "Let's not play games. I know who you are, and you know who I am."

I nodded reluctantly. "I know you're the man who master-minded the robbery at the National Gallery of Art."

He chuckled. "Mastermind? I love that word. I wish it were true. No, that fact you have wrong. That's why I had you brought here. So we could set the record straight and you could tell your friends at the FBI they are looking for the wrong person."

He started to roll up his sleeves and I could see the collection of tattoos on his forearms. One was a red-and-black eel that I recognized as the symbol of the Eastern European League, a crime syndicate known as EEL. There were other assorted tough-guy phrases and symbols, but one of them didn't fit in with the others.

It was a daisy with the numbers "24/7" directly beneath it. It looked like the logo of a flower shop willing to make deliveries twenty-four hours a day, seven days a week. But Nevrescu didn't exactly seem like a florist.

He saw that I was staring at it. "What's wrong, Little Sherlock?"

"*Young* Sherlock," I corrected.

"What's that?"

"They don't call me *Little* Sherlock. They call me *Young* Sherlock."

He laughed. "I thought you had no idea what I was talking about."

I gave him a look. "I thought we weren't playing games."

"Okay. So what's wrong, Young Sherlock?"

"I'm not sure but it's right there," I said, trying to make sense of it. "I can almost see it."

I closed my eyes and tried to picture the puzzle pieces: Daisy, 24/7, EEL, FBI, Nic the Knife, Romania, Happy Leprechaun, Safeway. It just didn't make sense and then . . . *SNAP*.

I opened my eyes and smiled. The solution seemed completely impossible except for one detail. It was the only thing that made the pieces fit together.

"There's been a huge mistake," I said urgently. "You need to let me go right now."

"Is that so?" He laughed. "Why should I do that?"

I looked right at him and did not blink. "Because the FBI is going to be here in less than five minutes and that doesn't leave us much time to talk about why your tattoo changes everything."

2.

The Meaning of TOAST

Three Months Earlier

I PROMISE I'LL EXPLAIN HOW NIC THE KNIFE'S
tattoo changed everything. But before I can do that, I have
to explain what *everything* is. That means I have to go back
three months earlier to when I first came to Washington.
Back then I wasn't a covert anything, just a kid whose family
moved a lot. And I wasn't looking for a criminal mastermind. I was trying to find my underwear.

"Mom!" I yelled down the stairs. "I can't find my boxers!"

You'd think that after four moves in seven years I'd be
better at packing and unpacking my stuff. But after dump-
ing three boxes of clothes onto my bed, I'd found plenty of

sweaters, jackets, and gloves (very helpful considering it was the middle of summer), but no underwear (unless you count an old pair of tighty-whities that were two sizes too small). It had reached the point where I'd had to put on a bathing suit after my shower.

"Mom!" I tried again.

There was still no response so I went looking for her. I was halfway down the stairs as I called out, "Do you know where my boxers . . ."

My words trailed off when I saw that she was at the front door talking to a girl. The last thing I wanted to do was discuss my underwear in front of some random girl, so I tried to make a save.

"Boxes," I said with a fake cough, trying to cover the change. "Do you know where my boxes are?"

Judging by the girl's smile, I had fooled exactly zero people.

"Florian, I'd like you to meet one of our new neighbors," Mom said. "This is Margaret."

The first thing that stood out about Margaret wasn't that she's African American or even that she's about three inches taller than me. It was that smile. Bright white teeth with silver braces across the bottom row. There was something so easy and friendly about it. I've always wanted a smile like that.

In pictures mine just looks like I'm scared of some creature lurking behind the camera, but hers radiated confidence.

"Welcome to the neighborhood," she said, holding up a plate of cookies.

"Thanks," I answered. "I was just looking . . . for . . . my . . ."

"Boxes," she said.

"Right, boxes."

There was an awkward silence until Mom came to the rescue. "Why don't I find them while you two have some cookies," she suggested. "In the kitchen, where there's less mess."

Margaret and I snaked our way though the unpacked chaos of the front room into the kitchen.

"Milk?" I offered.

"Yes, please."

Rather than sit down at the table, she poked around the piles of stuff stacked on the counter, more curious than snooping. "So where'd you move from?"

"Rome," I said.

She looked up. "The one in Italy?"

"Is there another?" I asked.

"I think there's one in Georgia," she said.

"It definitely wasn't Georgia," I replied. "It had the

Colosseum and lots of Italian people riding around on scooters."

"Is that where you always lived?"

"No. Before that we were in Boston, London, and Paris," I said. "We move a lot. My parents work in museums."

"That sounds cool. Mine are just lawyers," she replied as she plopped down at the kitchen table. "The boring kind, not the murder-trial kind. By the way, I love this house."

"Thanks," I said as I handed her a glass of milk. "I think yours is great, too. My mom's insanely jealous of the flowers in your front yard."

The instant I saw her reaction I realized my mistake and wished I could rewind the conversation and try it again.

"You know where I live?"

I stared at my cookie for a moment before nodding. "Four doors down and across the street. The yellow house with the brick chimney and a piano next to the big window in the front room."

She tilted her head to the side and asked, "How did you know that?"

I could have just told her that I saw her in her yard or something, but I didn't want to start with a lie. So I told her the truth. "Well, I saw the house. And just now I saw you. And I could tell that you live there."

"You could? Do I look like I live in a yellow house? Like I have a chimney and a piano?"

"Of course not," I replied. "It's just that I went for a walk this morning and . . ."

"You saw me then?" she asked.

"No, I'm pretty sure you were asleep."

"What time was it?" she asked.

"Five."

"I was definitely asleep. Do you normally go for walks that early?"

"Not *normally*. But we just got here a couple days ago and my body still thinks it's on Italy time. I woke up and couldn't fall back asleep, so I figured it would be a good opportunity to get to know the neighbors."

She laughed. "And how many neighbors did you meet at five in the morning?"

"None," I replied. "But I don't really need to meet them in order to get to know them. You can tell a lot about someone just by what you see from the sidewalk."

"And you were able to tell that the yellow house with the brick chimney and the piano is mine?"

I nodded.

"How?"

Past experience had taught me that people are turned

off by this particular skill. But I was too far along to stop now.

"There's a girl's bicycle in the side yard," I explained. "The seat is set high for someone tall, like you."

"Just because there's a girl's bike, that doesn't mean—"

"I'm not done," I said, cutting her off. "You're wearing a University of Michigan T-shirt and there is a University of Michigan Law School decal in the window of the silver station wagon in the driveway. There's also a DC Dynamo sticker on the bumper and an identical one on the bumper of the green sedan parked on the street."

"So?"

"Your soccer shorts," I said, pointing to them. "It says 'DCD' right there on your shorts. I'm guessing you play for the Dynamo."

She took another bite of her cookie as she thought through it all.

"Anything else?"

"Well, judging by the way you dip your cookie in your milk, I'd say you're left-handed. But that's about it."

She sat there for a moment with her mouth slightly open.

"That's amazing," she finally said. "I don't know if it's superfreaky amazing or unbelievably cool amazing. But it's definitely amazing."

"Usually people just think it's strange and they never talk to me again," I said. "But it would be great if you think it's cool because, from what I saw, only two other houses in the neighborhood have kids and they're way too young. You're my best bet for a friend."

"Is that so?" she said. "And did you do this with all of the houses in the neighborhood?"

I nodded.

She had a spark of an idea and I could see the wheels turning as she leaned forward and asked, "Which house belongs to the insane person who screams at you if you so much as put one toe in her front yard?"

"Easy," I replied. "Three doors to the left, blue house with the crazy perfect hedges."

"Who puts up way too many Christmas decorations?"

"Gray house across the street from you."

She gave me a look. "How could you possibly . . ."

"You can see the nails along the roofline where they hang the lights," I explained.

"Okay, let me come up with something you can't figure out from the street." She flashed an evil smile. "Where would you find a ridiculously large comic book collection?"

I toyed with her for a moment to let her think she'd stumped me. Then I answered, "The green house on the corner with the double security bars on the basement windows and the Fantastic Four license plate holder on the car."

At this point even I thought I was weird. But she just smiled and shook her head.

"I want that," she said. "I. Want. That."

"The comic book collection or the license plate holder?"

"No, that skill," she said. "Can you teach me how to do that?"

It had never dawned on me that this was something I could actually share with someone else. "You want me to teach you TOAST?"

"Toast?" she asked. "You've tasted my cookies, which are . . . epic. Don't you think I know how to make toast?"

"Not that toast," I said. "'TOAST' stands for the Theory of All Small Things. That's how I read people and places. The idea is that if you add up a bunch of little details, it reveals the larger truth."

"And where did you learn this theory? Philosophy class? Spy school?"

"I . . . invented it . . . I guess."

This made her laugh. "You invented TOAST?"

"It's based on some things I learned from my parents," I said. "But I put it all together and came up with the name. So yes, I invented it."

"You said your parents work at museums, right?"

"My father designs security systems, and one day he explained that the key to his job is finding the tiny flaw or inconsistency that the bad guys can take advantage of."

"Like the saying that 'a chain is only as strong as its weakest link'?"

"Exactly," I said. "And my mother's an art conservator. She restores old paintings and says the best way to understand a painting is by finding the smallest detail that tells the whole story, like the smile on the *Mona Lisa*."

"And this led to TOAST?"

I nodded. "Even though their jobs are incredibly different, they both rely on the idea that tiny things can be hugely important," I explained. "Once I even used TOAST to help my dad catch a criminal."

"This I have to hear," she said as she grabbed another cookie and chomped happily. "How'd you do that?"

"There was a museum in Spain that was robbed three times in a year. The stolen items were small but extremely valuable. No one could figure out how the thief was doing it. They hired my dad and he checked everything out and was just as stumped as they were.

"But one day he had a bunch of reports spread out on the kitchen table and I started looking at them. Most of it was technical stuff that I didn't understand, but I noticed all the robberies had two traits in common."

"What?" she asked eagerly.

"They all happened on Saturdays when it was raining."

Margaret considered this for a moment. "And you were able to figure it out from Saturday and rain?"

"No," I said. "I just noticed it. My dad was the one who figured it out. You see, museum attendance usually doubles on the weekend."

"That makes sense."

"And with that many people when it was raining, the coatroom didn't have enough space for all of the raincoats. They had to open an additional room to handle the extras. When they did that, they shut off part of the alarm system to keep it from sounding all day."

"That's brilliant," she said.

"Dad's pretty smart," I replied.

"And you'll teach me this?"

"Sure," I said. "But it will have to be some other time."

"Why?"

"Because I think you have to go somewhere right now."

"What time is it?" she asked, suddenly panicked. "I've got to get to soccer practice." She got up to go, and then stopped in her tracks and looked back at me.

"How did you know that?" she demanded. "Did you just TOAST me again?"

I laughed. "It's not a verb. But no, I didn't TOAST you. I can see the driveway through the side window. And your car just got here. My guess is that the woman headed to the front door is your mother."

Just then the doorbell rang.

"See you later," Margaret said as she rushed out of the room. When she reached the front door she turned back and added, "By the way, in case you're wondering whether I think it's cool or freaky?"

I took a nervous breath.

She flashed the smile and said, "Very, very cool."

3.

Napoleon's Candle

THERE ARE SOME THINGS, LIKE BREATHING AND walking, that you do automatically. And since you don't really think about them, they're hard to teach. For example, how would you teach somebody to breathe? Would you make up a list of step-by-step instructions?

1. Suck air through nose

2. Blow air back through nose

3. Repeat twenty thousand times every day

That might work, but it's kind of cheating because "suck air" and "blow air" are just two other ways of saying "breathe." You haven't actually explained how to do it. You've just swapped the words.

TOAST is like that for me. It's more instinct than idea. So when Margaret asked me to teach her, I wasn't sure how to break it down into something that made sense. I took her to the National Gallery of Art, the museum where my mom works, and showed her a painting of a man with red hair and a beard.

"Margaret, I'd like to introduce you to Vincent van Gogh," I said.

"Hey, Vince, how's it going?" she replied, playing along. Then she turned and asked, "Why do you want me to meet him?"

"Because he's the artist I know best," I told her. "Mom's crazy about him, so she's taught me a lot. Like for instance he only painted for about ten years but still created more than two thousand works of art."

"That's pretty amazing."

"And he usually couldn't afford to hire models, which is why he painted so many self-portraits, like this one. I love the colors: the orange beard, the blue background, the little flecks of green in his face."

Margaret studied the picture. "It's very cool, but he looks kind of sad."

"I think he was sad a lot of the time," I said.

"Is that why he cut off his ear?" she asked.

"How'd you know about that?"

"Everybody knows Van Gogh cut off his ear," she said. "It's common knowledge."

"I guess it is," I said. "But here's the funny thing: Everybody's wrong."

She gave me a curious look. "He didn't cut it off?"

"Maybe he did. Maybe he didn't. It's hard to say. But let me introduce you to someone else." I led her to a self-portrait on the opposite wall. "This is Paul Gauguin."

"Okay, this guy looks shady," she said.

"What makes you say that?"

"Because he's got a halo over his head, but he's holding a snake. So which one is he? An angel or a devil? A hero or a villain?"

"He might be a villain," I replied. "There's a chance *he's* the one who cut off Van Gogh's ear. They lived together and fought all the time. Gauguin loved to fence, and sometimes he'd grab his sword in the middle of an argument and threaten Vincent. The theory is that one time he did and accidentally cut off the ear with his sword."

"If that's what happened, why didn't Van Gogh tell any-body?" she asked. "Why did he let everyone think he'd done it to himself?"

"He worshipped Gauguin, so maybe he was embarrassed about what happened. Or maybe he wanted to make sure his friend didn't get into trouble. All we know for certain is that they never saw each other again after that night."

Margaret considered this. "It's interesting, but like you said, maybe he did or maybe he didn't. It's just a theory. If you can't know for sure, then you can't say that everybody's wrong."

"I don't think everybody's wrong because they *believe* Van Gogh cut off his own ear," I tried to explain. "I think they're wrong because they're *certain* he cut off his own ear. Once you're certain about something, you no longer question it. And if you don't question what you think you know, then you'll only ever see the big things and TOAST is worthless to you."

"Let me get this straight," she replied. "You're saying that big things, like everybody believing something, block the important details from view."

"Exactly," I said. "And now that you know that, we can get started."

We walked across the hall and I showed her a large

portrait of Napoléon standing in his study. "Okay, here's Napoléon," I said. "What time is it?"

"That's easy," she said, looking at the grandfather clock in the picture. "Four thirteen."

"A.m. or p.m.?"

She scrunched up her face and thought about it for a moment before saying, "I don't know."

"See if you can figure it out," I said. "Use TOAST."

It took her a minute, but when she did she flashed an aha smile. "A.m."

"How do you know?" I asked.

"Because the candle's lit," she said. "It's the middle of the night. Four a.m."

"That's TOAST," I told her. "Now let's try it out on some living people."

The museum turned out to be the perfect place to practice. It was filled with different types of people, so we had a broad cross-section to study. And they all moved slowly, which gave us plenty of time to observe. We started with a couple in the Rembrandt room. The woman had on a black dress, and the man wore a shirt and tie.

"What can you tell me about them?" I whispered as we stood across the room.

Margaret looked and answered quickly, "Both in their

twenties. She's got brown hair and is about five foot four. He's got black hair and is almost six feet tall."

"Let me rephrase that," I said. "What can you tell me . . . that isn't on their driver's licenses? Ignore the big things. What does TOAST tell you?"

She looked again, but after thirty seconds she turned to me, frustrated. "You know, if I already knew how to do it, I wouldn't need you to teach me."

"Fair point," I said. "How about if I ask you some questions?"

"Questions might be helpful."

"Is there anything that doesn't seem like it belongs?"

"You mean like their clothes?" she asked.

"What makes you say their clothes don't belong?"

"They're dressed for work, not for sightseeing."

"That's good," I told her. "Build on that. Do you think they work here at the museum?"

"No," she replied. "Because they're walking around and looking at the paintings like visitors, not employees."

"Give me another detail that stands out."

She looked some more and replied, "Her shoes. She's wearing a nice dress, but with sneakers. They don't go together."

"That's very good," I told her. "You've got two small

things that don't seem to fit. When you add them together, what do they tell you?"

She thought about it for a moment. "She takes the Metro and walks to work. She wants to be comfortable and she doesn't want to scuff up her nice shoes, so she keeps those in her office and wears the sneakers whenever she leaves. I bet they're on their lunch break."

"Look at that. You're a natural."

Margaret smiled. "Want to know more?"

"Sure," I said.

"Judging by their age, they're probably interns. She wanted to come and look at the pretty pictures. He wanted to come and look at the pretty girl."

I laughed. "What makes you say that?"

"Notice how she's looking at the paintings. She's wrapped up in them. But he's turned toward her."

She was absolutely right.

"Like I said, you're a natural."

We did this for another hour, going from room to room, picking up on little details and clues about people, before ending up where we started, by the self-portraits of Van Gogh and Gauguin. There we came across a man who'd nodded off to sleep while sitting on a couch, which made him an ideal subject. He wasn't moving, which made him easy to study. And his eyes were closed, so he couldn't see us looking at him.

"Ready to take a test?" I asked.

She smiled confidently. "Ready to take it. Ready to crush it."

"Find out everything you can about Sleeping Beauty and meet me over there by Gauguin."

"It's in the bag," she replied.

I walked by him first and pretended to look at a Degas painting of ballerinas. While I did, I made some mental notes about him. Margaret was more direct. She actually sat at the other end of the couch and got a close-up look.

She stayed there for a minute and then came over to me. I was smiling because of her bold move, but she seemed unhappy.

"What's wrong?" I asked.

"I was doing great up until now, but I didn't notice anything interesting or out of place about him," she explained. "The only thing close is that he's got a scar on his chin. Does that mean anything?"

"Just that he cut himself once," I said.

"That's what I figured."

"You want me to ask you some questions like before?"

"I don't want you to," she replied. "But I guess I need you to."

"Sometimes it's not so obvious," I said. "You've got to

start small and build up. Can you tell me anything about where he lives?"

She started to give me an "are you crazy?" look, but then she realized something.

"Not in DC," she said. "He's wearing a T-shirt from the Spy Museum and he has a big, bulky camera on a strap around his neck. He's a tourist. That means he doesn't live in Washington."

"Good," I said. "So that's where he doesn't live. Do you have any idea where he does?"

"No," she said, stumped. "Do you?"

"He's from Europe. Of course, it's easier for me because two weeks ago so was I."

She turned to look back at him, and this time she saw it. "His shoes! His running shoes look funny!"

"You got it," I said, signaling her to lower her voice. "Those are called Europa trainers. They're a brand from Eastern Europe. They don't sell them in the States."

"That's cool," said Margaret. "I'll do better with the next one. Give me another test."

"We're not done with him."

"We're not?" she asked. "What else can you tell?"

"He's wearing contact lenses, he's left-handed, and he's here with his wife and baby."

"You can't possibly know that." Then she gave me a look. "Can you?"

"There are indentation marks on the bridge of his nose and on both temples that could only be made by wearing glasses on a regular basis. But there is no sign of them today, so he's wearing his contacts. There are spit-up stains on his shoulder, the kind you get from holding a baby. And since we determined that the shirt is a souvenir from the trip, it's most likely the first time he's ever worn it. That means the stains are fresh and the baby is with him today. The wedding ring tells us that he's married. The fact that he's wearing his wedding ring on the right hand is another sign that he's European, probably Eastern European. It's more of a custom there. My guess is that they're a couple making their first trip with their baby, which would explain why he's so tired."

"And how do you know he's left-handed?"

"The spit stains from the baby are on the right shoulder," I explained. "That's the side that a left-handed person would use. You're left-handed; how would you hold a baby?"

Margaret thought about this for a second and imagined she was holding a baby. Her instinct was to hold it on her right shoulder.

"It's clever, I'll give you that," she said. "But you can't be sure. It's all still guessing."

"Yes, but it's informed guessing. The whole point of TOAST is that one little thing can be misleading, but the more little things there are, the more likely the guesses are to being right. Like the shoes *and* the wedding ring both being Eastern European."

Just then a woman carrying a baby approached the man and started talking to him in a language neither of us recognized. He smiled as he placed the baby against his right shoulder and started to pat its back with his left hand. Margaret continued to watch them as the couple shared a quick kiss and started to walk together through the museum.

"One day I'll be able to do that," she said.

"What?" I asked. "Burp a baby?"

"Very funny," she replied, slugging me in the arm. "No, one day I'll be able to read people like that. Like you do."

A week later Margaret was over at my house and Mom was making her special Sunday spaghetti sauce. It's a legendary family recipe that simmers all day and fills the house with the most amazing aroma.

"That smells incredible, Mrs. B.," Margaret said as we passed through the kitchen.

"Thank you," she said. "Would you like to stay for dinner?"

"To eat that?" replied Margaret. "I would *love* to stay for dinner."

"Check with your parents," said Mom. "Florian's dad is on his way home from the airport, so we should be eating in about an hour."

Dad had been on a business trip for most of the week. When we sat down to eat, he hadn't even had a chance to tell us anything about it before Margaret asked him, "Did you have fun playing golf while you were in California?"

"I had a great time," he said, "but I played awful."

She nodded and replied, "Well, it's hard to play well when you're using somebody else's clubs. At least that's what my dad says."

She tried to play it cool, but when she turned and saw my expression, she couldn't help but break into a huge grin.

"How did you know my father had been to California?" I asked. "And how did you know he played golf when he was there? I didn't even know that, so I couldn't have told you."

"And how could you have possibly known that I used someone else's clubs?" asked Dad.

She was still beaming as she looked at our stunned faces and said, "I just used TOAST."

4.

The Copyist

WE SAT IN SILENT AMAZEMENT UNTIL MY MOTHER began to laugh.

"At last," she said gleefully. "Someone has done to Florian what he does to us."

I laughed too. I couldn't believe it. Margaret had used TOAST to figure out that my father borrowed someone else's golf clubs during his trip to California. And I had absolutely no idea how. I kept looking back and forth between Dad and her, trying to figure out what clues she saw.

"You better tell him how you did it," Dad said. "Before his brain explodes."

"Please do," I said. "I'm completely stumped."

Margaret basked in a moment of glory before she explained. "First of all, the trip to California. I knew that before we even sat down. Mr. Bates put his briefcase on the hall table and there's a copy of the *Los Angeles Times* sticking out of the pocket." She turned to my father. "I'm guessing you read it on the flight home."

"I sure did," he told her. "That's good."

"Okay, but that's not enough," I said, holding up a hand to call time-out. "Just because he has a newspaper doesn't mean he was there. We get the *New York Times* every Sunday without going to New York. The *LA Times* is for sale in airports all over the country."

"True, but TOAST is about multiple small things," she replied. "And you didn't let me finish. There's also a claim tag on the briefcase's handle. It says LACMA."

"Lacma? What's that?"

"I don't know, but I'm pretty sure the LA stands for Los Angeles," she said. "Maybe the Los Angeles Contemporary Museum of Art."

"Los Angeles *County* Museum of Art," said Dad. "They're my new clients. I spent the last three days studying their security protocols."

"So that gets you to California," said my mother. "How did you know he played golf?"

"His hands gave it away."

Dad held them up, and I saw it instantly.

"His right hand is tan and his left hand is pale," I said, shaking my head. "How could I miss that?"

"Yeah, Florian, how could you miss that?" asked Mom. Then she turned to Margaret and whispered, "What did he miss?"

"You only wear one glove when you golf," she explained. "If you play enough in a short period of time, the sun only tans the one exposed hand."

Mom gave Dad a suspicious look and asked, "Exactly how much did you play while you were *studying* their security protocols?"

He grinned. "Is it my fault the museum director loves to play golf and discuss work at the same time?"

"It still doesn't explain how you knew he borrowed clubs," I said.

Margaret smiled. "That was the easiest part of all. We were all here when he came home. He had a suitcase and a briefcase . . ."

". . . but he wasn't carrying golf clubs," I said.

"Nope. That means he had to borrow some while he was out there."

It was brilliant. Actually, it was better than brilliant.

It was perfect. Margaret had taken my special thing and turned it into our special thing. Up until that moment the real value of TOAST was that it helped me figure out new things whenever my family moved. But that was the day it became something different. From that point on it became something the two of us could do together.

For example, when we rode the Metro we'd play a game where we'd try to predict who was getting off at which stop based only on what they were carrying. And one time we sat on the steps of the Lincoln Memorial and tried to figure out what state different tourists were from by the clothes they were wearing. The more we played, the better we got. But we weren't trying to develop our skills so that we could become detectives or spies or anything like that. We were just having fun.

Until we saw him.

It was July 29. I remember it because it was Margaret's birthday. As a present, my mom had arranged for us to go behind the scenes at the museum. She took us into the studio where she works, showed us all the high-tech equipment, and even let us see a newly acquired Picasso that hadn't gone on display yet. It was very cool and when we left we walked through the Impressionism galleries.

That's where we came across an artist painting a replica of Monet's *Woman with a Parasol*.

"Is he a conservator like your mom?" asked Margaret.

"No," I replied. "He's a copyist."

"You mean like a forger?"

"It's only forgery if you say it's the original," I explained. "Copyists are artists who practice by painting copies of other works. It's a great way to learn from the masters. It's how most great artists got started."

"So he doesn't work here?" asked Margaret.

"No, but he had to get a permit from the museum," I said. "I doubt it was hard because he's really good. His painting looks just like the original. "

"European too," said Margaret.

"French, to be precise," I said. "It's a Monet, *Woman with a Parasol*."

"Not the painting," she replied. "I mean the artist is European. Check out his shoes."

He was wearing Europa trainers like the man we saw the first day I taught her about TOAST.

"Just like Sleeping Beauty," she continued.

I started to laugh, but then something caught my attention. The man we saw the first day was a young father on vacation. This man was an artist hard at work. If you stood them side by side, they'd look almost nothing alike, but the Theory of All Small Things led me to an unexpected conclusion.

"I think it's the same guy," I said.

"No way," said Margaret. "He was blond and this guy has black hair."

"I know."

"And he was a total tourist," she added. "Not a hipster art student."

"I know that, too. But I still think it's him."

"Why?"

"For one, look how he's painting: He's left-handed, just like the other guy."

"A lot of people are left-handed," she replied as she held up her left hand and wiggled her fingers. "Like me, for example."

"Only ten percent of people are left-handed," I said. "If you multiply that ten percent by the small number of people in Washington who have those shoes, and narrow that group down by men that age with that body type, the number gets ridiculously small. Then consider that they were both in this museum during the last few weeks, and it says that he's the same person we saw before."

"You're telling me that you trust TOAST more than you trust your own eyes?" she said. "The small things tell you one thing and you go with that?"

I thought about it for a moment before I answered.

"I do," I said. "I absolutely do."

She sighed. "So do I. I can't put my finger on the exact reason why, but he seems like the same guy to me, too. I wish there was a way we could tell for sure."

"Yeah," I replied, lost in thought.

We stood there for a moment, and then we both turned and looked at each other at the exact same time and said, "The scar."

"It's on his chin," she said. "And you remember who spotted that scar, don't you?"

"I believe it was you."

"Oh, you don't believe it was me," she teased. "You know it was me. You thought it was worthless, but I thought it was important. Turns out . . . I was right."

"So what's the plan?" I asked. "You want to stand here and keep congratulating yourself? Or do you want to go look for the scar?"

"I'm all for doing both," she answered. "But I guess I could take it easy on you and we could just go find out."

I figured we'd casually look at some nearby paintings and glance at his chin, but Margaret's approach was more direct. She walked right up to him and leaned over his shoulder.

"Your painting is beautiful," she said.

"Thanks," he replied with a trace of an accent. "It helps to have something beautiful like a Monet to copy."

As he talked he turned to look at her and smiled. The scar was right there across the left side of his chin.

Neither of us had any doubt. It was the same man.

5.

Foggy Bottom

"WHAT SHOULD WE DO?" MARGARET ASKED urgently.

"What do you mean?" I replied.

"Should we call the police? Alert security?"

"And tell them what?"

We'd moved into the massive hallway that runs through the middle of the National Gallery, so we could keep an eye on the copyist without him hearing us.

"We'll tell them that the man in there is not who he is pretending to be," she said in an excited whisper.

"He's not pretending to be anyone," I said. "He says he's a copyist, and judging by his painting, that's exactly what he is."

"Then he's a forger," she said. "He's making a forgery of *Woman with a Parasol* to sell on the black market. Where do you think the black market is for paintings like that? Paris? Cairo? Marrakech?"

"Definitely Marrakech," I answered with a laugh. "Except it doesn't make sense to forge a painting that's on public display. No one would be fooled because all they have to do is go online to see that the original is hanging in the museum."

"I got it. I got it. I got it," she said excitedly but still trying to keep her voice down. "He's a spy. No, even better, he's an international hit man. That makes total sense."

"How in the world does international hit man make total sense?"

"He completely changed his appearance," she said. "That means he's hiding something. Hit men hide stuff. It's like the main thing they do. You know . . . other than kill people."

"I've created a monster," I said, shaking my head. "Maybe I should have warned you sooner, but there's a trap that comes with TOAST. And I think you've fallen into it."

"What trap?" she asked.

"Crazy conspiracy theories," I said. "Just because something is unexpected doesn't mean it's suspicious. Most things are completely innocent and can be easily explained. If you think about it, all he's done is change his hair. Have you ever changed yours?"

"Yes, but . . ." She let out a sigh and slumped a bit. "Why are you trying to take all the fun out of this?"

I laughed. "You think it would be fun if he actually was an international hit man?"

"Maybe 'fun' isn't the right word," she replied. "But you know what I mean. You're the one who taught me TOAST and all I'm doing is using it."

"Yes, but you're using it to make wild speculations," I said.

"Okay," she said. "Forget hit man. Forget forger and spy. Just tell me that you honestly don't think he's suspicious and I'll let it go."

I studied him through the doorway as he started to pack up his paints and brushes for the day. It was definitely the same guy and he looked really different. . . .

"Okay," I admitted. "He's a little suspicious. But we can't call the police or tell security that they need to arrest someone because he changed his hair. I'm pretty sure they'd want evidence of something . . . you know . . . criminal."

"I completely agree," she said to my momentary relief. Then she added, "So let's find some and give it to them."

"Find some what?"

"Evidence," she replied. "Let's follow him and see where he goes."

I thought she was joking, so I waited for her to laugh. But the laugh never came. She was serious. "That's the worst idea ever," I told her.

"Why?"

"First of all we don't know how to follow people," I responded. "We play games with TOAST. That doesn't make us spies. Also, what if he actually is a bad guy and he catches us? That would be monumentally bad."

"He's not going to catch us," she said. "I guarantee it."

"And you're so confident because . . ."

"We're going to follow him with TOAST," she answered.

"What does that even mean?" I asked with a raised eyebrow.

"We don't actually follow him; instead we make him follow us," she replied. "We read him and figure out where he's going and we get there before he does. He can't see us behind him if we're out in front."

"You mean like predicting who gets off the Metro at which stop?" I said.

"That's exactly what I mean. You see that plastic bag he's putting his supplies in?" she asked.

I looked over at him. "Sure."

"The logo is from the George Washington University

bookstore. If he's a student and lives near campus, then he's going to get off at the Foggy Bottom Metro stop. So let's get there first and keep an eye out for him."

I hesitated before answering. She'd gotten my interest, but it still sounded dangerous.

"Don't forget that it's my birthday," she reminded me. "This can be your present to me."

"I already gave you a present," I said in mock protest. "And the most dangerous part was the potential for a paper cut while gift wrapping."

"If there's anything just a little bit dangerous, I promise we'll call it off, go back to my house, and have some cake."

He was almost packed up. The copyists store their equipment in a room downstairs, so I knew this was our only chance to pull off her plan.

"Come on," she added. "Let's have an adventure."

"Adventure" was the part I couldn't resist.

"Okay," I said. "But only because it's your birthday. *And* I still want a piece of cake."

Thirty minutes later we were sitting on a bench on the edge of the GWU campus drinking sodas to fight the summer heat and keeping an eye on the exit of the Foggy Bottom Metro station. And thirty minutes after that, we were still waiting.

"How long before we give up?" I asked, only half joking.

"We're not going to give up," she replied. "This will work. We just have to be patient."

"Aren't you supposed to go out for birthday dinner with your parents?"

"I've got an hour," she said, checking the time. "That means we can wait twenty more minutes and I'll still have enough time to get home and get ready."

"Are you going someplace fancy?" I asked.

"The exact opposite. We're going to Ben's Chili Bowl. It's a hamburger-and-hot-dog place over on U Street. We go every year on my birthday."

"That's cool," I said. "We don't have any places that are traditions like that. We've moved too much."

"Not me," she replied. "I've lived in the same house my whole life." Then she hesitated for a moment and added, "Well, except for the first couple weeks."

"What do you mean?" I asked.

Margaret took a sip of soda and thought about her answer.

"Actually . . . I'm adopted," she said somewhat carefully. "We don't know the specifics of where I came from. We're not even sure if today is my actual birthday. It's just the one we picked to celebrate. My birth parents abandoned me at a firehouse when I was about ten days old. Engine House Four."

This caught me completely off guard. I think it was because she used the word "abandoned." It was so cold and sad. I sat quietly for a moment before saying, "It's amazing that one person could be so unlucky and lucky in the same week."

"How do you mean?" she asked.

"So unlucky to have parents who would do that," I explained. "So lucky to end up with the ones you did."

The corners of her mouth turned up into a tiny smile and she looked over at me. "Thanks." She took another sip and was about to say something else when we caught a glimpse of our guy coming out of the Metro station.

"There he is," I said.

He was alone and in a hurry. We froze for a second, surprised that the plan had worked.

"Don't get up," I whispered. "You talked to him earlier, so he's seen your face. Just look at me."

She turned toward me and I watched him. He got as close as twenty feet before jogging across the street.

"Okay, you can look now," I told her.

We followed him, staying across the street and about fifteen feet behind him as he walked. My pulse started racing.

He turned onto H Street and entered a ten-story brick building with a sign that read PHILIP S. AMSTERDAM HALL. It was one of the GWU dorms.

"So now we know he's a student," she said.

"Which is still not evidence of anything criminal," I countered.

"True, but we're not done yet."

"We're not?"

She shook her head. "I've still got ten more minutes before we have to leave."

We crossed the street and approached the dormitory. We tried to open the door but couldn't without a pass card. The windows were tinted, so we cupped our hands over our eyes and pressed up against the glass to see better. A flyer on the door advertised summer housing orientation.

"I think we should go," I said.

"Just give me a second," she said. She rapped her knuckles against the glass and turned to me saying, "I just want to peek inside."

She rapped again.

We were about to give up when someone opened the door.

Margaret started to say thank you but stopped when she saw it was the copyist. He looked at her with a hint of recognition.

"Do I know you?" he asked.

"No," she answered, her voice cracking.

"Actually, I think we've seen you before," I said, trying to think fast. "We were down here in the lobby the other day waiting for my brother. He lives on the fifth floor."

He looked at me for a moment and slowly nodded. "That must be it."

He held the door open for us to enter, but we were way too scared to move.

"Aren't you coming in?"

"No," I said, trying not to sound nervous. "I was just looking to see if my brother was inside. But he's not. We'll wait out front."

"Yeah," Margaret added. "Thanks."

He shrugged and said, "Okay."

He disappeared into the building, and after about twenty seconds of standing still (whether we were keeping cool or momentarily paralyzed by fear is open for debate), Margaret and I bolted toward the Metro station. We were still breathing heavily when we got on the train and plopped down into our seats. I didn't feel any relief until the doors closed and I knew he hadn't followed us.

"Okay," Margaret said. "That was officially the dumbest idea ever."

I was too shaken to speak so I just nodded my agreement.

6.

The Scene of the Crime

OVER THE NEXT TWO WEEKS MARGARET AND I avoided the National Gallery so we wouldn't bump into the copyist. We also decided not to tell security (because we didn't have any evidence) or our parents (considering following a stranger across town would definitely get us grounded). Instead we kept our *adventure* to ourselves and focused on the fast-approaching first day of school.

With all the times my family had moved, I'd developed strong new-kid survival skills. Normally I used TOAST to find pockets of potential friends and avoid the jerks and bullies. But Margaret gave me something new: advanced intelligence. She told me about the different cliques, her favorite teachers, and what foods to avoid in the cafeteria. (Pretty much all of them.)

We even went on a scout. Her soccer team played on the field behind the school, so one day I went to practice. Afterward she introduced me to some of her teammates in our grade, and then we looked around the campus. The main building was huge: three stories of red brick with large columns at the front entrance. It was intimidating, and when I looked through a window down an endless hallway of lockers, I wondered if I'd feel lost there.

That same night my dad's ringtone woke me at 2:17. I would've gone back to sleep but when I heard him talking I could tell it was an emergency. I worried about my grandfather, who'd been sick, and wondered if there'd been a turn for the worse.

I sleepily staggered out to the hallway just as Dad hurried toward the stairs, still buttoning his shirt as he rushed.

"Is everyone okay?" I asked. "Something wrong with Grandpa Ted?"

"Grandpa's fine," he said. "I didn't mean to wake you."

"Where are you going?"

"Three paintings were stolen from the National Gallery and they want my help. Go back to sleep."

He was halfway out the door before my semiconscious brain made the connection.

"Wait!" I called out.

"I can't, buddy, this is important. We can talk in the morning."

"Were they Impressionist paintings?"

The door closed and I figured he didn't hear me. But then it slowly opened and I saw him standing there looking up the stairs at me, his head haloed by the porch light.

"Why do you ask that? What makes you think they were Impressionist?"

I took a deep breath and sighed. "I may know something."

"I don't have time for games, Florian. Something like what?"

Awkward pause.

"Like, I may know who did it."

He gave me a confused look.

"Margaret and I noticed this strange guy hanging out at the museum. . . . We kind of followed him."

"You did what?" he exclaimed.

"Yeah, I know, it was stupid," I replied. "But he was suspicious. And he was hanging out in the Impressionism section."

Dad was in too much of a hurry to analyze the whole

situation, so he trusted his gut. "Get dressed quick. I'll tell your mom you're going with me and leave out the part about you following a suspicious man across town. We'll deal with that later."

"Good idea," I said. "Although, we don't really have to ever tell her that part, do we?"

In normal traffic it takes about thirty-five minutes to get from our house to the museum. But with the streets empty, we made it in twenty. That gave me just enough time to tell Dad everything I knew about the man in the Europa trainers.

He slowed down when we turned onto Constitution Avenue and the museum came into view.

"This is going to be a zoo," he said. "An absolute zoo."

As we got closer, we could see security officers setting up wooden barricades along the sidewalks and news crews unloading camera gear from television trucks. Everything was bathed in the red and blue lights of the police cars that clogged the road.

The entrance to the underground parking lot was blocked by it all, so we parked down the street in front of the Smithsonian's Museum of Natural History and walked.

Dad flashed his security credentials at the checkpoint and we climbed the massive steps that led to the entrance.

"They're looking for clues," he said, nodding toward

some cops who were shining their flashlights into the bushes along the front of the building.

Everything was surreal.

We entered the main rotunda and the first thing I saw was a pair of detectives questioning the cleaning crew. The custodians looked nervous, as if the giant pillars that circled them formed a marble holding cell.

"You think they're witnesses or suspects?" I asked.

Dad just shrugged and said, "Good question."

I looked back over my shoulder as we continued walking, trying to make sense of it all. Skylights normally gave the hallway a bright, sunny feel, but now there were sinister shadows and pockets of total darkness.

We stopped to look into the room where Margaret and I had seen the copyist painting *Woman with a Parasol*. The plaque on the door read IMPRESSIONISM/GALLERY 85, but the entryway was blocked by bright yellow police tape. Inside, the crime scene unit searched for evidence around the huge gap on the wall where a painting had been.

"Wow," said Dad when he saw the empty space. "Just wow!"

"What's missing?" I asked.

"*Child with Toys*," he answered. "Renoir."

"Unbelievable," I said under my breath.

We could see through to more activity in another gallery.

"The other two were taken from there," he said. "*The Dance Class* by Degas and Van Gogh's *Girl in White*."

"Renoir, Degas, and Van Gogh," I said, shaking my head. "This guy isn't messing around."

"No, he isn't," said Dad.

We took an elevator three floors underground to the security center. Although the marble and limestone made the rest of the building feel like a Roman temple, this room looked like it belonged in a science fiction movie. All the furniture was black leather and silver metal, and the wall was covered with a bank of monitors playing surveillance video from throughout the building.

Two people were already there: a man in the corner with a British accent talking on a phone and another furiously typing away on the main computer console. The British man, wearing black jeans and a stylish black T-shirt, tried to sound calm but looked anything but as he paced back and forth.

"No, sir, I'm on top of things," he said unconvincingly. "We'll have it under control."

The man at the computer looked up and saw my father. "Jim, I'm glad you're here."

He was heavyset with a big moon face. His pale skin and

the circles under his eyes made it look like he hardly ever slept or stepped out into the sun. His jacket and tie had been tossed aside and his overall vibe was rumpled wreck.

"I want you to look over the data from the . . ." he stopped when he noticed me. "Who's this?"

"Earl, this is my son Florian," Dad said. "It's a long story, but . . ."

He didn't get time to explain. The door flew open and two more people stormed in. One was Serena Miller, the director of museum security and an old friend of Dad's. I recognized her because she'd stopped by the house to visit the first week we were in Washington. The other was a tall African-American man wearing a dark blue suit with a matching tie. Unlike Earl, his suit was still crisp and pressed. And unlike the British man, he wasn't trying to *appear* calm. He was completely cool and composed.

"Jim, this is Special Agent Marcus Rivers of the FBI's art crime team," Ms. Miller said, introducing him to my father.

"Nice to meet you," Dad said, shaking his hand.

"This is Jim Bates," she said, continuing the introduction. "He consults with us and I've asked him to help and . . ." Like Earl, she stopped the moment she saw me. "And for some reason he's brought along his son."

Rivers looked at me, more curious than angry, and then

turned to my dad. "It's not exactly a bring-your-kid-to-work kind of situation, is it?"

"I'm sorry about that," Dad replied. "But I think he may have seen something . . . *interesting* and I thought you should hear it."

"Interesting?" he asked. "In what way?"

"Tell them," Dad said to me. "Be as specific and accurate as possible."

Everyone was staring. Even the British man, who'd now finished his phone call. It was an intimidating group, especially considering there was a special agent in the mix. I took a deep breath and just started talking.

"About four weeks ago, my friend Margaret and I saw a man asleep on one of the couches in the gallery with Van Gogh's self-portrait. He was a tourist with blond hair. He slept for about fifteen minutes until his wife and their baby joined him."

They looked confused, but I just kept talking. "Then two weeks ago, we saw a copyist painting a replica of Monet's *Woman with a Parasol.* He had dark hair and was dressed like an art student. A total hipster. He goes to George Washington University and lives in the Philip S. Amsterdam Hall. I point that out because that residence hall does not allow married students or children. Married students are housed somewhere else. I checked online."

This was when the British man spoke up. "What's the point of this?" he asked impatiently. "Sixty-five million dollars in art is missing and we're listening to a child recount insignificant information. I've just had a very unpleasant phone call with my bosses back in England and assured them we are acting swiftly."

I ignored him and focused on the agent. "The sleeping father and the artist were the same man," I said. "A man who'd decided to completely change his appearance."

"Are we seriously letting this continue?" asked the Brit. "Every second we waste is a second the thief gets farther away."

"Why do you think they're the same person?" asked the agent.

"Both were wearing Europa trainers, a type of running shoe found only in Eastern Europe. Both were left-handed. And both had identical scars on their chins. I don't think it was the same person, I'm certain of it."

He obviously did not know what to make of me.

"Oh, and another thing," I said. "The two rooms we saw him in. Rooms in which he spent long periods of time. They're the same two rooms that just got robbed."

That's when the agent smiled. "Well, now. That does seem interesting."

7.

Seen but Not Heard

AGENT RIVERS WAS INTRIGUED BY MY STORY OF the man in the European shoes. But as far as clues and potential leads went, it was way down the list. It had been two weeks since Margaret and I had seen the man, and the museum was an active crime scene with fresh evidence to be gathered and security footage to be viewed.

Rivers let me stay because every copyist has to apply for a permit. When there was a free moment, he planned to have someone get the applications so I could look at the ID photos and see if any belonged to the man. Until then I was supposed to sit in the back of the room and wait.

Silently.

The silent part was stressed more than once, but I didn't mind. I had a front row seat to an actual mystery and my father was one of the good guys trying to solve it. It was beyond cool. I listened carefully as they re-created the events of the night.

"Start at the beginning," Rivers instructed. "How did someone take three paintings without setting off an alarm?"

"Our security software is all being updated," Ms. Miller explained. "Earl was in charge."

"That's right," he said. "We have fixes every few months, but this is the first major overhaul in years. The entire system had to be taken off-line while it rebooted. That meant we had no cameras, motion sensors, or alarms. We were totally dark."

"There are supposed to be countermeasures when you do that," said the British man.

"There were," answered Ms. Miller. "We overlapped shifts so we had extra guards along the perimeter of the building during the upgrade."

"And they didn't see anything?" asked Dad.

"Nothing out of the ordinary."

"I'm sorry," interrupted the agent, looking at the British man. "Who are you again?"

"Oliver Hobbes," he said. "I'm with the insurance company."

"And were you here during the reboot?" he asked.

"No, they called me after the paintings were found missing," he said.

"And when was that?" the agent asked.

"The system went down at one fifteen and everything was back up and running at one thirty-two," said Miller. "A custodian noticed a painting was missing and sounded the alarm at one fifty-one."

Rivers wrote down the times in a notepad he carried.

The mention of the custodian reminded me of the scene in the rotunda when we arrived. I scanned the monitors and saw that the police were still questioning the cleaning staff. There were five custodians waiting by the fountain while two others were talking to detectives off to the side. All of them wore matching blue coveralls. Their work carts were lined up in two rows of four on the far wall. I wished the monitors had sound so I could eavesdrop.

On another pair of monitors I saw the crime scene unit looking for evidence in the rooms that had been burglarized. I was amazed by how meticulously they worked. Then something struck me, and I looked back at the screen showing the rotunda.

There were two rows of four work carts, which made a total of eight, but there were only seven workers. Someone was missing. I checked the other monitors, looking for any-one else in blue coveralls.

There were none.

"Dad," I blurted out excitedly. "Dad!"

The conversation at the table stopped abruptly and everyone glared at me.

"You really need to be quiet, Florian," my father said impatiently. "We have to focus on this."

"One of the custodians is missing," I said, pointing at the monitor.

"What do you mean?" asked Agent Rivers.

"There are eight carts but only seven custodians," I explained. "Where'd the extra cart come from?"

The agent walked right up to the monitor and tapped each person on the screen as he counted. Seven. He didn't say a thing. He just bolted out of the room with Serena and Earl right behind him.

That left me alone with my father and Hobbes, the insurance agent. Dad came over and sat next to me.

"I'm sorry," I said. "I know I wasn't supposed to talk, but . . ."

"It's okay," he assured me. "That was great that you noticed it . . . although maybe not so great for them."

On the screen we could see Rivers pull the detectives

aside and start a heated conversation. Once again I wished there were sound on the monitors.

"I owe you a huge apology," Hobbes said as he approached and offered his hand. "I was stressed and upset and I took it out on you. I hope you can forgive me."

"Of course," I said. "It's pretty crazy having a twelve-year-old interrupt your crime scene. I probably would have reacted the same way."

"Oliver Hobbes," he said as we shook.

"Florian Bates," I replied. "You said you work with the insurance company, right?"

"Yes," he answered. "The museum called me right after they called your dad."

"Oliver and I have crossed paths often," said my father.

"Yeah, your father's one of the best in the business," he replied. "I was relieved to see that he's part of the recovery team."

Before we could continue the conversation, Agent Rivers and the others returned. "What's your name?" he asked as he strode back to the main console.

"Florian Bates," I replied.

"How old are you?"

"Twelve."

"Well, twelve-year-old Florian Bates, you are officially

smarter than the detectives of the Metropolitan Police Department. They had no idea they were missing a custodian." He turned to Ms. Miller. "Can you pull up the security video starting at thirty minutes before the robbery?"

"Of course."

She nodded to Earl, who sat down and started typing. Within seconds the monitors were filled with footage from earlier in the night. The time on the bottom of each image read "12:45."

"What are we looking for?" asked Dad.

"A guilty-looking custodian," said the agent.

Even sped up, the footage was incredibly boring.

We were about halfway through it when Hobbes shook his head and complained, "They're all the same size. They're wearing identical uniforms. And they're looking down, not up at the cameras."

"I didn't say it would be easy," replied Rivers. "What were those shoes you were talking about?"

It took me a moment to realize he was asking me.

"What?" I asked.

"You said he had on a special type of shoe," he replied. "If he's our guy, he may have the same shoes on in this picture."

I hadn't even thought about that.

"Brilliant," said Oliver. "Check the shoes."

For the first time I moved over from the couch and stood next to them, examining each pair of shoes on the screen. First it was exciting. Then it was nerve-racking. And finally, it was embarrassing. We went back and forth over an hour and a half's worth of security footage and there was no sign of the man in the Europa trainers. I was so certain we'd find him. I was certain I'd be a hero. My clue was a dud.

"I guess I was wrong," I said softly.

"Don't sweat it," said the agent as he put a friendly hand on my shoulder. "I still want you to look through the applications to see if you can identify him. You never know how these things come together."

I forced a smile and nodded.

"Look there," said my dad, pointing at one of the monitors. "Who's that?"

The monitor showed the exterior of the building as a man in a blue custodian's uniform crossed Constitution Avenue and disappeared into the darkness.

"I think that's our eighth custodian," said the agent. "What's the time?"

"One forty-three," answered Earl.

"What time does the custodial shift end?"

"Not until four," he replied.

Agent Rivers turned the knob to make the video play

in reverse and stopped it at the point where we had the best view of the custodian. It still wasn't much to go by. His back was turned to the camera and he was wearing a baseball cap, so we couldn't really tell anything about him.

"So I've got a question," said Rivers. "If that's our guy leaving the scene, then where are the paintings?"

8.

Nightcrawlers

IT WAS NEARLY FOUR IN THE MORNING BUT THE
National Gallery was anything but sleepy. Since the prime
suspect left with nothing in his possession, everyone was
scouring the building to see if the paintings had been hidden in the museum. Everyone, that is, except for me and
Earl.

We stayed in the security center, where he worked on his
computer and I waited for my mom to pick me up. The mystery man in the Europa trainers was now even farther down
the list of leads. I was being sent home.

"Did you have to stay in here just to keep an eye on me?"
I asked. "If so, I'm really sorry."

"No," he said. "I'm responsible for the software upgrade and I need to keep an eye on the network while it filters through the entire system. Besides, you shouldn't apologize for anything. You saved the day."

"You think so?"

"Absolutely," he said.

"Thanks, Mr. . . ."

"No Mr.," he replied. "Just call me Earl."

I smiled. "Okay. Thanks, Earl."

"This is some show we've got tonight, isn't it?" he asked, looking at the security monitors.

On the screens we could see teams of police officers, security guards, and detectives hunting for any place the paintings could be hidden. There were people on ladders poking up into the ceiling tiles. There was a crew taking apart the couches in the galleries. A lot of attention was focused on bathrooms as well as the storage areas not open to the public. Agent Rivers was in charge of it all, and he marched up and down the main hallway giving orders and conferring with my father and Ms. Miller.

"If he hid the paintings here, that means he has to come back to get them," I said. "That seems really dangerous."

"Maybe not as dangerous as walking across the street

with them under his arm," said Earl. "He's obviously smart, so he must have figured out some way to get them without getting caught."

"And if he's smart, he must have picked those paintings on purpose," I reasoned. "Something like that wouldn't be random."

He gave me a look and smiled. "I've been thinking the same thing all night."

He typed something into the computer and the basic information about each of the three paintings came up on the screen in front of us:

The Dance Class by Edgar Degas (c. 1873)
Oil on canvas, 18 3/4″ x 24 1/2″
Gallery 83

Girl in White by Vincent van Gogh (1890)
Oil on canvas, 26 1/4″ x 18 1/16″
Gallery 83

Child with Toys by Auguste Renoir (1895–1896)
Oil on canvas, 21 3/8″ x 25 3/4″
Gallery 85

"What do they have in common?" I asked.

"The Degas and the Renoir are both French Impressionism," he said. "*Girl in White* is technically Postimpressionism. But most people don't notice the difference."

"Wow," I said. "You really know your art."

"I've spent eight of the last ten years trying to protect every painting in this building," he said. "After a while you get to know them pretty well."

"Why only eight?" I asked.

"I worked across the street at the National Archives for two years," he said. "But I missed this place too much and begged Serena for my old job."

"Since you know the paintings so well, can you think of why someone would want these three in particular?"

He shook his head. "Not really. They're not even the most valuable pieces in the rooms they were in."

"According to Mr. Hobbes, they're worth over sixty-five million dollars," I said.

"Don't get me wrong, they're incredibly valuable," he said. "But if you're going to risk stealing masterpieces, why not take the *most* valuable or at least the most important works?"

It was a good point but I reminded myself that monetary value and historical importance were big things, which can be misleading. I thought about the small things. I thought about TOAST.

I looked at the images on the computer and tried to figure out what small things they had in common. The Renoir was a picture of a young boy and his nanny playing with toys. The Degas showed ballerinas in a dance class. And the Van Gogh had a woman in a dress walking through a field of flowers. No common themes.

I looked at the years they were painted, their previous owners, and even the frames they were in. They still had nothing in common. I was stumped until I noticed one seemingly insignificant thing.

"They're the same size!" I said.

"What?"

"They're all within a couple inches of being the same size," I said, not sure why it would be important.

Before I could come up with anything more, my mother arrived. Since she worked at the museum, her security pass let her come right in and pick me up.

"I can't believe this really happened," she said, looking at the monitors as she entered the room.

"They stole three paintings," I said. "Renoir, Degas, and Van Gogh."

"That's what your dad told me on the phone," she said,

her eyes still fixed on the monitors. "I just can't imagine."

"Florian was a big help," Earl said. "I think without him they still wouldn't have any idea what happened."

She smiled. "Well, thank you. But I think it's time that I take him home so he can get some sleep."

"Can't we stay just a little bit longer?" I asked. "I know you're just as curious as I am."

"That's not the point," she said. "They've got work to do. I'm sure your dad will fill us in on everything."

I said good-bye to Earl and we left. As we rode the elevator, I asked her, "Why would someone steal a painting because of its size instead of its value?"

"I don't know," said Mom. "Maybe the criminal has small walls and there's not enough room for bigger paintings."

We both laughed at this.

But it kind of made sense. Maybe there was some sort of size limit. I didn't figure out what it could be until we were in the rotunda and I saw the crime scene unit examining the extra work cart. That's when I noticed that unlike the others, its trash bag was empty.

"That's it!" I said to Mom. "Where's Dad?"

"What's it?"

"I know where the paintings are."

I remembered my father had been walking up and down

the main hall with Rivers. I started running toward where I'd seen them last.

"Wait for me," called Mom, trying to keep up.

I found them by the fountain in the East Garden Court. The first one to see me was Agent Rivers. Rather than being angry, he seemed amused.

"Let me guess?" he said. "You've solved the case?"

"I–I think so," I stammered, trying to catch my breath.

This caught him off guard, and I realized he'd been joking.

"All the paintings are about nineteen by twenty-five inches," I said.

"Okay," he said. "Why does that matter?"

"It's the perfect size to fit in his trash bag. That's how he went from room to room without anyone noticing. The paintings were in his trash bag on the cart. And that's how he's getting them out of the building."

"They're in the trash!" exclaimed Rivers.

"So he doesn't have to come back for them," I responded. "The garbage truck will pick them up for him."

"Where's trash collection?" he asked Ms. Miller.

"Right this way," she said, pointing.

Everyone rushed out to a loading dock, where there were three large Dumpsters, two blue and one green. Even though it was the middle of the night, a truck was backing up to pick up a blue one. It turns out that a lot of the city's garbage is collected at night, when the tourists and government officials are gone.

"Stop. Right. Now," Rivers said, holding up his badge. "Nobody move."

A very dedicated team of FBI agents spent the next thirty minutes digging through the Dumpsters and bags of trash while detectives questioned the garbage crew to see if they might be involved. They didn't find anything until they checked the green recycling Dumpster.

All three paintings were found tucked in a stack of cardboard boxes that had been folded and bundled together. The size was the key. If they were just a few inches bigger they wouldn't have fit in the bundler.

"Twelve-year-old Florian Bates," Agent Rivers bellowed. "You are not just smarter than the officers of the Metropolitan Police Department. You are smarter than all of us."

My mom and dad laughed, but the strangest thing happened. The searchers all turned to me and gave me a round of applause.

I'd never felt anything like it before.

9.

Sunday Sauce

I WOKE UP WITH MY HEAD AT THE WRONG END OF the bed, completely unsure if the "4:15" on my clock was morning or afternoon. It was just like I was in Napoléon's portrait, only there were no candles to help me solve the mystery. The most disorienting part was the amazing aroma that filled the air. It was the unmistakable, mouthwatering smell of my mom's Sunday spaghetti sauce. But this was Saturday. Or at least I thought it was. There was a decent chance I'd slept for an entire day. Either that or I was having a smellucination. (Is there such a thing?)

"Mom?" I called into the kitchen as I walked down the stairs.

"Ah, look who's awake." Her hands were busy grating Parmesan cheese, so she bypassed the hug and leaned over to give me a kiss on the forehead. "Hello, sleepyhead."

"It's not Sunday, is it?" I asked, a bit nervous.

"No, it's still Saturday," she replied to my relief. "I figured I'd break with tradition and make your favorite meal a day early. You know, because you're such a good son. Oh, and the part about you saving over sixty-five million dollars in art from being stolen didn't hurt."

I smiled. "That really happened, huh? I thought maybe I had dreamed it."

"No, it happened," exclaimed a voice.

I turned to see Margaret sitting at the table, a big, goofy grin on her face.

"It's all over the news and I have been waiting all day to hear the inside story," she continued.

"Hey, Margaret, when did you get here?"

"After my game."

It was only then that it registered she was wearing her DC Dynamo soccer jersey. "Oh, wait! Today was the play-offs. Did I miss it?"

"Just by a couple hours," she said. "And it's a shame, because I was amazing. In fact, the reason I came over was to give you a hard time for missing it. But then your mom told me about what happened and I figured it was an acceptable excuse. Barely acceptable. But acceptable."

"Did you win?" I asked.

"Four–nothing, remember the part about me being amazing?" she said. "But we can talk about soccer later. I want to hear about the robbery. It's all over the news, but there hasn't been anything about a twelve-year-old boy as part of the story. Start at the beginning. You know, right after the part where I had to convince you the copyist was suspicious and worth looking into. Start there."

I laughed and began to fill her in on what happened. I told her about arriving at the crime scene and telling the FBI about the copyist. I went through the details of the missing janitor and the search for the three paintings. I explained it all, and by the time I got to the discovery of the paintings, she and my mother were on the edge of their seats. (Mom had heard only bits and pieces of it before I went to sleep.)

"Mom and I were about to leave when I finally realized the importance of the size of the paintings," I said.

"I still don't get that part," Margaret said.

"They had to be small enough to fit into the garbage bag on his cart," I explained. "But more important, they had to fit into the machine that bundled all the cardboard boxes together for recycling. It was a great plan because the boxes provided padding to protect the paintings from getting hurt. And the recycling truck would have actually taken them out of the museum. All the thief had to do was wait for them to be delivered at the recycling center."

"That. Is. Amazing," Margaret said. "After they found the paintings, did they catch the guy who stole them? Did they find the eighth janitor?"

"Actually . . . I don't know. I've been asleep. Mom?"

"Not yet," she answered. "Your dad said the FBI set up a stakeout at the recycling center, but he didn't show up. He's still out there somewhere."

That made me happy they hadn't mentioned me on the news. I was part of the reason someone lost $65 million. He was mad and the last thing I wanted was for him to even know I existed.

"So who's hungry?" asked Mom. "I think we should go ahead and eat without your dad. There's no telling when he'll get home."

The spaghetti was delicious (of course), and while we ate I tried to fill in any gaps I may have left in the story. We also got Margaret to tell us all about her soccer game, which on any other day would have been the big news.

"Does that mean you're in the WAGS championship?" I asked as I twirled some pasta onto my fork.

"We play the final next week," she said. "And I better see you there."

"I wouldn't miss it," I said. "Unless of course the FBI needs any more help with international art crimes."

"What's WAGS?" asked my mom.

"Washington Area Girls Soccer," explained Margaret. "It's made up of leagues all over the District. There are about a hundred teams in our division."

"And you're playing for the championship?"

Margaret nodded and smiled.

"That's impressive," said Mom.

Just then the front door opened and my dad hurried into the house. "Hello," he called out.

"In here," said Mom. "Sorry, we started without you. We didn't know when you'd get home."

"Actually, I'm just here for a second," he replied as he came into the kitchen. "I'd like you to meet someone."

"Hello, Mrs. Bates," said the man following Dad. "I'm Special Agent Marcus Rivers of the FBI. We didn't get a chance for an official introduction last night."

"Well, you had a lot going on," Mom joked as she stood up and shook his hand.

"He's the agent in charge," I whispered to Margaret.

Despite the fact that he probably hadn't slept at all, Agent

Rivers still looked as sharp as he did the night before. The only difference was that he'd switched from the dark blue suit to a dark gray one.

"Would you like to stay for dinner?" asked my mother.

He took a deep whiff and practically swooned. "I'd love nothing more, but I'm in something of a fluid situation at the moment." He turned his attention to Margaret and me. "Florian, is this the friend you were with when you saw the man in the museum?"

"Yes," I said. "This is Margaret."

"Nice to meet you, Margaret," he replied. "I don't mean to be rude, but how can I get in touch with your parents?"

"My parents?" she asked. "Am I in trouble of some kind?"

"Of course not," he said. "It's just that you're a minor and I'm going to need them to be involved."

"I think they're at the grocery store," she said. "But they should be back in half an hour."

Rivers checked his watch and looked back up at her. "Actually, we don't have that much time. Why don't we call them there?" He handed his phone to her. "Just dial the number."

"What's going on?" I asked him.

"I need you both to come down to the Hoover Building."

"What's the Hoover Building?" I asked.

"FBI Headquarters."

10.

The Bureau

MARGARET WAS EXCITED. HANDS-IN-THE-AIR-ON-a-roller-coaster excited. Except instead of whizzing around a theme park, we were racing down Massachusetts Avenue.

"This is so cool!" she exclaimed as the agent behind the wheel expertly maneuvered in and out of traffic. "Imagine if you could get to school this way. You'd never get another tardy."

"No, but you might get whiplash," I replied as my fingers gripped my armrest. (Did I mention that I hate roller coasters?)

We were riding in a government-issue black SUV with an armored body and bulletproof windows. "It's not like anyone's going to shoot at us," Rivers assured us when he told us about these features. "That's just how they come."

After we'd wolfed down the rest of our spaghetti while he spoke with Margaret's parents on the phone, Margaret raced home to change. Then we all piled into the vehicle. Mom and Dad sat in the back row, Margaret and me in the middle, and Rivers in the passenger seat, while another agent drove.

Fast.

Apparently, FBI agents don't have to follow the speed limit when they're on a case.

"Look, look, look!" Margaret said, pointing at a tourist holding up her phone to take a picture. "She's taking our picture. She thinks we're important." Margaret smiled and waved even though the tinted window made it impossible for the woman to see her.

"Why exactly are we going to the Hoover Building?" I asked.

"Two reasons," said Rivers. "I want you two to look at some pictures to see if you recognize the man you saw in the museum."

"I. Told. You. So," Margaret said, poking me in the shoulder to punctuate each word. "He's an international hit man. Couldn't be more obvious."

"Actually, he's not," replied the agent. "But he may be involved with some high-end art crimes. That's what we're trying to figure out."

"What's the other reason?" asked my mother.

"Admiral Douglas wants to personally thank Florian for his help last night," he said. "We're going to stop by his office."

"Admiral Douglas?" I asked. "Who's he?"

"Admiral David Denton Douglas is the director of the FBI," explained Rivers "He's a close adviser of the president and as powerful as they get. In all his years as director, this is the first time he's ever requested a meeting with an eleven-year-old."

"Hey," I protested. "I'm twelve."

Rivers laughed.

"I'm just messing with you," he said. "I know all about you, Florian Bates. You were born at Brigham and Women's Hospital in Boston, Massachusetts, on March twenty-fourth to parents James and Francesca Bates. Most recently you attended the Castelli International School in Rome, where you got straight As except for a B in physical education."

"How do you get a B in PE?" asked Margaret.

"It's a long story," I said with a sour face, unhappy to be reminded of what I considered a miscarriage of academic justice.

"And you will soon be starting seventh grade at Alice Deal Middle School," Rivers continued. "Where you'll be part of the International Baccalaureate program. Very impressive, by the way."

"How do you know all that?"

"The I in FBI, it stands for 'investigation,'" he said. "We know things. Besides, you're about to meet the director. We don't let that happen without a thorough background check."

"Well, just for the record, it's not certain that I'll be in the IB program," I told him. "I've applied for it but won't find out if I was accepted until next week."

"Okay," Rivers replied. "Maybe I wasn't supposed to say anything about that. Just act surprised when they tell you."

Margaret and I shared a happy look. She was already in IB and this meant we'd have classes together.

"What about me?" she asked playfully. "Do you know anything about me?"

Agent Rivers opened an e-mail on his phone and started reading. "Margaret Campbell. Daughter of Paul and Denise Campbell. Both attorneys. Also a student at Alice Deal Middle School." He looked up from his phone. "Favorite color: purple."

She was blown away. "The FBI knows my favorite color?"

He shook his head. "No, I looked at the purple shirt,

the purple sneakers, and the purple nail polish and took a guess. With regard to the other stuff, I called it in as soon as Florian told me your name."

The SUV pulled into an underground parking structure where an agent was already waiting. He gave us visitor badges and within seconds we were on an elevator. I wasn't sure if we were in a rush because we were on a tight schedule or if the Bureau wanted to make sure no one saw us there.

We got out on the fifth floor, which was a maze of offices and cubicles. Because it was a Saturday, most were empty, but there were some people scattered about.

"Working on a Saturday," Margaret said. "That's just not right."

"Yeah, well, we haven't had much luck convincing the criminals to take the weekends off, but we're trying," he joked. "This area is all dedicated to major theft investigations. Cargo Theft over there. Jewelry and Gems next to that. And this is Art."

"Your office," I said.

"Home sweet home."

A few minutes later, Margaret's parents were ushered in and we all sat down on a pair of couches. Each family on a different couch with the kids in the middle.

"Now that we're all here, I'd like to officially welcome

you to the Hoover Building," Rivers said. "And I'd like to thank you for doing this on such short notice."

"Sure," said Margaret's dad. "But what exactly are we doing?"

"Margaret and Florian reported seeing a suspicious person at the National Gallery. We want to show them a photo array to see if they can identify that man."

"Is this dangerous?" asked her mother.

"Not at all," he said. "One of the reasons we're doing this on a Saturday in my office is because that way they'll be nowhere near anyone who might identify them. We're not asking them to testify in court. We've just received some surveillance footage and we want to know if we're looking at the right guy."

The four parents all shared some concerned looks but nodded their agreement.

"Great, let's start with Margaret," he said. "Why don't you and your parents come with me, while the Bates family waits here? I don't want your identification to influence Florian's."

They left the room and I sat there with my parents.

"This has been a crazy twenty-four hours," Mom said under her breath.

"You're not kidding," replied my father.

Normally, you can tell a lot about a person by looking at their office. But all I could tell about Agent Rivers was that he's neat. Extremely neat. The only personal touch on his desk was a picture of him at a graduation with his parents and a younger sister. His mom and dad looked proud. His sister looked bored. Other than that, there was no hint as to what his life outside of law enforcement might involve. The shelves of his bookcase were filled with neatly organized art books, and the walls had an impressive display of diplomas. He had a bachelor's degree from Harvard and a master's and PhD from Georgetown. No wonder his parents looked so proud.

It took less than two minutes for them to come back to the room. "All right, Florian. Your turn."

My parents and I followed him into a large room near his office.

"We call this the bullpen," he said. "It's where we brainstorm different cases."

The room had a few tables and large marker boards on each wall. Each board had information about a different case. On one board there were pictures of the interior and exterior of the National Gallery, diagrams of the crime scene, copies of each of the three paintings, and a timeline of events.

"We call this a case board," he explained. "It's where we put what we know about a case so we can all be on the same page. You see that empty space there?" he asked.

"Yeah," I said.

"That's where we'd like to have a photo of our prime suspect," he explained. "Hopefully you'll be able to help us with that."

"I'll do my best," I replied.

"I know you will," he told me. "I'm going to show you six photographs and I want you to tell me if any one of them is the man you saw at the National Gallery. Don't tell me what you think I want to hear. Don't tell me something that you *think* you might remember. Only tell me what you are exactly certain of. Understand?"

I nodded. "Yes, sir."

He put a binder in front of me and opened it to reveal two rows of three photographs. It took me all of a second and a half to point to the one in the lower right corner.

"That's him," I said. "That's how he looked the first time we saw him. When he had blond hair and a wife and a baby."

"Are you certain?"

"Without a doubt," I assured him.

"That's exactly what Margaret said."

He smiled, peeled the photo off the paper, and taped it in the empty spot on the case board. "There now, doesn't that look better?"

"It sure does," I said.

He told us to wait while he got Margaret and her parents. When they entered, she smiled the second she saw the picture taped to the case board. She knew that meant I'd identified the same person. Rivers logged on to a computer and turned the monitor toward us.

"Now I want to show you some security footage from Dulles International Airport," he said. "Tell me if you see the man again."

He pressed a key and a slideshow of images began to play. Each shot was a picture of someone going through airport security. Each one stayed up for about a second and a half. We watched carefully, trying to make sure we didn't miss anything.

"That's him," both of us said at the exact same time.

Rivers hit the space bar and stopped the slideshow so the picture froze on the screen. In this image, the man looked like he did the second time we saw him, with dark hair. He had a kind, innocent face.

"Are you certain?" asked Rivers. "He looks like a completely different person."

"There's no doubt," I said.

"That's how he looked when he was a copyist," added Margaret. "I know it's him."

"Go back two pictures," I said.

Rivers gave me a curious look, but did just that, stopping at a picture of an older man going through security.

"Look," I said, pointing at the background of the image. "You can see his feet when he was waiting in line. You can see the Europa trainers I was telling you about."

Rivers smiled. "Okay. I'm convinced."

He opened a file and referenced it while he talked to us. "We believe his name is Pavel Novak. He's from the Czech Republic and is thought to have been involved in several art crimes in Eastern Europe. We've had no record of him ever coming to the United States before, which is how we missed him."

"But he's the guy, right?" said Margaret. "He dressed up as the eighth janitor and stole the paintings."

"Actually, no," said Rivers. "These pictures were taken yesterday afternoon, about ten hours before the burglary. When the paintings were being stolen, he was in an airplane over the Atlantic Ocean."

We mulled this over for a moment.

"Are you sure?" I asked.

Rivers nodded. "That doesn't mean he wasn't involved.

He almost certainly was. He just wasn't the one who stole the paintings from the wall."

"If he didn't steal them, then what did he do?" I asked.

"My guess is that he was studying the museum, trying to get a solid feel for everything from schedules to security. Because of you, we know he was in both rooms where there were paintings stolen. That's a huge help."

"But when he was in the gallery with the Van Gogh and the Degas, he was asleep," I replied. "What could he see with his eyes shut?"

"He had a camera," said Margaret. "He had a big, bulky camera. He could have been shooting video the whole time he was pretending to be asleep. Then he could go back and look at it later."

Rivers smiled at Margaret and then her parents. "I guess only smart kids go to Alice Deal Middle," he said. "That's a very good theory."

"And we know he spent days in the other gallery while he was painting the copy of *Woman with a Parasol*," I added.

"Eight days total according to the copyist office," he said. "So now that we know Novak was the one you saw, we can start searching his known associates in Washington and among EEL."

"What's EEL?" asked my mother.

"The Eastern European League," he said. "It's a crime

syndicate with strong ties in the Czech Republic, Slovakia, Romania, and Bulgaria."

Margaret and I shook our heads in total disbelief. What had started out as a game, practicing TOAST, now involved the FBI and an international crime syndicate.

"What do we do now?" asked my dad.

"We just have to wait here for another twelve minutes," said Rivers, checking his watch. "Then we'll go up to the admiral's office. He keeps an exact schedule. Not a minute early, not a minute late."

I poked around the bullpen while we waited and looked at the case boards, including one where a man was taking down the pictures.

"Solved it?" I asked.

"More like decided it wasn't for us," he replied.

"This is Agent Crosby from Jewelry and Gems," Rivers said by way of introduction. "We go way back."

"If you're trying to catch someone smuggling diamonds from Sierra Leone, I'm your guy," he said to everyone.

Three pictures were taped to the board and numbered "1," "2," and "3." A date was written beneath each. There was also a map of Washington with corresponding locations marked with the same numbers. None of the locations were near each other.

"What's the case?" I asked.

"Three B and Es," said Agent Crosby. "That's breaking and entering. A sapphire ring was stolen from one. A pearl necklace from another. And we're not sure if anything was stolen from the third."

"A ring and a necklace?" I asked. "I know you're Jewelry and Gems, but that doesn't sound big enough for the FBI."

"It's not," he replied. "But all three victims are employed by the CIA. They asked us to look into it to make sure the cases weren't related. They aren't, so we're returning them to our friends in the Metropolitan Police Department."

I looked at the pictures and something caught my eye.

"Uh-oh," I heard Margaret whisper to my mom.

"What?" she asked.

"He just saw a clue they missed," Margaret said. "Watch this."

It wasn't really a clue yet, but there was something. All three photographs were taken in apartments. The first two in kitchens and the third in a bedroom.

I pointed to the open window in one of the kitchen shots. "Is that how the burglar got into the apartment? Through the window?"

Agent Crosby gave me a confused look, not sure why I cared.

"Yes," he said.

I studied the picture, and then the other kitchen shot.

"Can I see a picture from the third victim's kitchen?" I asked.

Now Crosby was annoyed. He was about to tell me it was none of my business when Agent Rivers joined the conversation.

"Why don't you show him?" he instructed. "Just for fun."

"The kitchen's not relevant," Crosby told us. "In that robbery, the burglar entered through the bedroom window."

"I'd still like to see it," I replied.

Rivers looked at me and smiled, which was the exact opposite reaction to Agent Crosby's.

"Show it to him," Rivers said a bit forcefully. That's when I realized he outranked him. Crosby dug through a file, pulled out a picture, and handed it to me. I saw exactly what I was looking for.

"Do any of these victims have anything to do with China?" I asked.

"As a matter of fact, two of them do," he said, surprised. "They work at the Chinese counterintelligence desk." He thought for a moment. "How could you possibly know that?"

"I think you better tell the CIA that the Chinese government is trying to spy on these employees," I said.

Rivers laughed and Crosby looked like he'd just been punched in the gut. Margaret walked over and put a friendly hand on his shoulder. "Don't feel bad. He does that to everyone. You just got TOASTed."

11.

The Admiral

I USED TO THINK THE PRINCIPAL'S OFFICE WAS intimidating.

Then I got called to the office of the director of the FBI and developed a whole new understanding of the word.

The reception area had dark paneling, antique furniture, and three massive paintings on the wall. The names beneath the paintings formed the motto of the FBI. There was *Fidelity*, featuring an eagle soaring over the Grand Canyon; *Bravery*, which showed a Civil War battle scene; and *Integrity*, with George Washington taking the oath of office.

This was the room where Mom, Dad, Margaret, and her parents sat waiting under the watchful eye of a man who politely offered everybody bottled water but also looked like he knew seventeen different ways to kill you with a pencil.

Agent Rivers led me into a room with a large desk and a conference table. In here, one wall was covered with a map of the United States. Another was filled with photographs of the director with various world leaders. And a third contained a hidden door that opened onto a smaller, secret office.

That's where the director and Rivers talked while I waited nervously, wondering what I had gotten myself into.

"I thought I was just supposed to thank him?" the director asked. "I didn't realize we were involving him in other cases."

"Yes, sir," said Rivers. "But I think you should listen to his theory. It's compelling. Especially when you consider that his last theory helped us recover more than sixty-five million dollars in stolen art."

They lowered their voices and I couldn't hear much more until the end of the conversation when he asked, "How old is he again?"

"Twelve," responded Rivers. "But not like any twelve-year-old you've ever met."

They walked into the room and I was surprised by how tall the director was. He stood at least six foot four and wore his silver-gray hair in a crew cut. He had a thin mustache that curled up ever so slightly at the ends, and his imposing presence was softened by the hint of a Southern accent.

"Florian, it's nice to meet you," he said. "I'm Admiral Douglas."

"It's an honor, sir," I replied as we shook hands.

"Agent Rivers says that you're some sort of superdetective. Would you say that's an accurate assessment?"

"Well . . . sir," I replied, flustered, "I don't know if I'd—"

"Son, in this room there's no need for modesty," he interrupted. "Just answer the question."

I took a breath and replied as confidently as I could manage, "I notice things that other people miss."

"What sort of things?" he asked.

It felt like a test. I knew Agent Rivers had put his reputation on the line and I wasn't about to let him down. I decided to show off.

"Well, sir, I know that you have a chronically sore back," I said. "And that you've owned that tie for more than a decade."

He checked to see which tie he was wearing and then looked at Agent Rivers for a moment before turning back to me and asking, "What makes you say that?"

"The only nongovernmental item in this room is the small pillow you keep on the bottom shelf of the bookcase behind your desk," I responded. "I assume you use it to give your back relief when you sit for long periods. Also, your laces are tied along the inner edge of each shoe rather than the middle. Instead of leaning over and tying them while they're flat on the floor, you put your foot up on your knee to ease the strain. Finally, there is a model of a submarine on the corner of your desk with an engraving thanking you for your service as its captain. Considering your height and the low ceilings on a sub, I imagine you had to bend over much of the time, which is probably when your back troubles started in the first place."

He smiled. "And the tie?"

"There's a photograph on the wall behind me of you meeting the former prime minister of France," I said. "You're wearing the same tie in the picture and he died twelve years ago. That means the tie is at least twelve years old."

Douglas laughed and turned to Agent Rivers, who flashed a huge smile.

"Not like any other twelve-year-old indeed," he said. "Florian, why don't we have a seat and talk about what the Chinese government is up to?"

We sat at the conference table and Rivers pulled three photographs from a file, placing them in front of the director and me.

"Three apartments, each the home of a CIA employee,"

said Rivers. "And each also the scene of a relatively small break-in."

Douglas looked at the pictures for a moment and asked, "And you think each of these was committed by a spy working for the Chinese government?"

"I can't be certain he's working for the government," I replied. "He could be working for a corporation or some other organization, but the government seems most likely."

"And what makes you think this?"

"TOAST, sir."

"I see three kitchens, son," he replied. "But no toast."

"TOAST is the Theory of All Small Things," I told him. "It's how I . . . well, for lack of a better term . . . it's how I solve mysteries."

This made him smile. "Seeing as I'm just the director of the FBI and not a superdetective, why don't you explain it to me?"

"TOAST considers small, seemingly insignificant details that when added together reveal hidden truths," I said. "In this instance, the three apartments are located in entirely different parts of the city. Each is at least four miles from the other two. Yet all of them have a menu from the same Chinese restaurant on the refrigerator. That's what caught my attention."

The admiral smiled at this detail. "That's interesting, but I hardly think that—"

"It says 'Free Delivery' on the top of the menu," I continued. "Do you know a Chinese restaurant that has free delivery throughout the entire city? Normally they only deliver in a one- or two-mile radius, a mathematic impossibility for these apartments."

"Good point," he replied.

"And if you notice, identical coupons have been torn off the bottom of each menu. You can still see part of one here. It says 'half off your first order.'"

I handed the admiral the picture for him to examine.

"Imagine that you're a spy who wants to infiltrate the CIA. You can't break into headquarters. You can't hack employee records on the agency's computer servers. You can't follow workers when they head home. All of these are overt acts that run the risk of getting caught. But you're completely safe if the employees invite you to their homes."

Admiral Douglas shook his head in amazement. "You get them to order food."

"That's right," I said. "Somehow the spy got these menus into CIA headquarters. Maybe he made a delivery to the building and just stuck a bunch of menus in with the food. Maybe he got someone to innocently bring them in. But somehow they made their way into a common area such as a break room where they were left out for anyone."

"And if only those menus have the coupon," said Rivers. "That means whenever anyone places an order and mentions the coupon, the person taking the call knows it's someone who works for the CIA."

I nodded. "So our spy delivers the food, and the person opens the door, allowing him to look inside the apartment, maybe even secretly take a picture or two. Later on he breaks in, makes it look like a burglary, and sneaks a listening device into a purse or briefcase."

Admiral Douglas looked at it all for a moment in total disbelief. "That's brilliant."

"He really thought of everything," I said.

He laughed. "I wasn't talking about the spy, Florian. I was talking about you."

This made me blush.

"How long have our men been working on this case?" he asked Agent Rivers.

"A couple of weeks," he replied.

"And how long did it take Florian to crack it wide open?"

Rivers smiled. "A couple of minutes."

"Mrs. Jenkins, can you come in here for a moment," Douglas called out to one of the secretaries. "Take-out

Chinese," he muttered to himself as he waited for her to come in. "Unbelievable."

A woman appeared at the door with a notepad in her hand.

"Yes, sir," she said.

"I need you to schedule an appointment with the director of the CIA and tell him it's urgent," he said. "And please ask Florian's parents to come in here. I'd like to discuss something with them."

I looked at Agent Rivers and he just shrugged, unsure why the director wanted to speak to my parents.

"Florian, just for fun, why don't you close your eyes?"

"Sure," I said.

"What color are my socks?" he asked. "Black or blue?"

"Neither, sir," I said with a smile. "They're burgundy."

He laughed again. "Thought I might trick you on that one."

Just then Mrs. Jenkins walked my parents into the room. Admiral Douglas jumped up from his seat and greeted them, giving each an enthusiastic handshake.

"Welcome, welcome," he said. "This is some boy you have here."

"We think so," said Mom.

"Please have a seat," he said, motioning toward the table.

"I'm going to be honest. I have to go to the White House this evening, and now, thanks to Florian, I also have to squeeze in a quick chat with the director of the CIA. So if you'll pardon me, I don't have time for any small talk. I'm just going to cut to the chase."

"Certainly," said Dad.

"I would like Florian to work with us here at the Bureau."

My eyes opened wide. "You want me to be an FBI agent?"

"Actually, I was thinking more as a consultant," he replied. "Not often. But every now and then we might call and ask you to do that TOAST thing. I still don't fully understand it, but I've only dedicated thirty-plus years to intelligence gathering."

"Mom? Dad? Can I?" I asked excitedly.

"He's joking," my father said.

"No, I'm afraid not," he replied. "The only thing crazier than me asking a twelve-year-old to join us would be me not asking. In two days he's helped us locate over sixty-five million dollars in stolen art and quite possibly uncovered a clandestine spying operation being run by the Chinese government. Imagine what he could do if we gave him another two days."

My parents were speechless, which I took as a sign that they were at least considering it.

"Would I get paid?" I asked.

The director chuckled at this. "We'd have to figure something out," he replied. "We can't put a twelve-year-old on the payroll without attracting congressional attention, but I'm sure there's a way we can compensate you for your services."

"In a college fund," blurted my mom. "We'll create a college fund and you can pay him there."

"That's a fantastic idea," said the director.

"But he can only help you when he's done with his homework," she continued.

"What's that?" asked the director.

"He can help save the country," she said. "But only after he finishes all of his schoolwork. I won't let this hurt his grades."

The director laughed. "Sounds reasonable to me. What do you think, Florian? You want to join us?"

It was the easiest question I ever answered.

12.

The New FBI

IT WAS WEDNESDAY MORNING AND MY PARENTS were at work. I'd just poured the milk on my cereal and was about to savor that perfectly crunchy first spoonful when the doorbell rang.

"This is going to change everything," Margaret announced as she entered the room tornado-style, midway through a conversation that had apparently started without me.

"What is?" I asked.

"My big idea," she answered as though it was obvious. "It's epic."

"Something tells me this isn't a brief conversation," I

replied. "Can you explain it in the kitchen? I don't want my cereal to get soggy."

"Kitchen it is," she said, trying to seem as accommodating as possible.

We sat at the table and I ate while she kept talking.

"I'm just going to say three words," she said. "The New FBI."

"What's the New FBI?" I mumbled, my mouth full of Alpha-Bits.

"Florian Bates Investigations."

I swallowed the cereal and smiled. "I get it. That's funny."

"It's not funny, it's brilliant," she said. "You're already a consultant to the actual FBI. This just takes it to the logical next step. As soon as word gets out about you, people will start knocking on your door looking for everything from stolen property to missing persons. Senators, ambassadors . . . spies. They'll come when they've run out of options because . . . Florian Bates Investigations is solving the mysteries of the world, one case at a time." (That last part she said with a ta-da kind of feeling.)

"You even came up with a slogan?"

"I told you it was epic."

"Except no one's going to come because word's not going to get out," I countered. "The only ones who'll know about me are the FBI, my parents, and you. Admiral Douglas and Agent Rivers didn't even want me to tell you, but I told them it was deal breaker. I said that you're my best friend and I wouldn't lie to you."

"You said that?"

"Of course I did," I replied.

"That's really sweet," she said. "But trust me when I say that nothing stays secret in Washington. It may just be passed along as a whisper or rumor, but people will find out. They'll find out because they'll be desperate. Because no one else will be able to help them. That's when they'll come looking for us."

"Us?"

"Yeah, us," she said. "I'm going to be your partner. You're great with clues, but let's face it, your people skills are lacking."

"What's wrong with my people skills?" I asked incredulously.

"That's the beauty of it. You don't have to worry about what's wrong with your people skills because I've got it covered," she said. "I'll also help you with the investigating. I've gotten pretty good at TOAST. If we work together, there's no mystery we can't solve."

"I can't tell if you're joking or not."

She gave me a look. "No joke. In fact, we've already gotten our first case."

"We have? Who's the client?"

Her expression changed and she forced a little smile. "Me."

"And what mystery do you want solved? Because if you want me to spy on the team you guys are playing in the finals I'm going to have to say no."

"It's nothing like that," she said. "I don't need your help to win a soccer game."

"Then what do you need it for?"

"I want you to find my parents. My birth parents. I want you to find out who they are and why they abandoned me at the fire station."

This caught me completely off guard and the mood took a sudden turn from silly to serious. I didn't know what to say.

"When we were in the SUV with Agent Rivers, he knew everything about you," she continued. "He knew your birthday. The name of the hospital where you were born. He knew your entire history. But he skipped over those parts with me. That's because even the FBI can't figure out where I come from. But you can, Florian. If anyone can do it, it's you."

"I think it's really dangerous," I said.

"No one's going to hurt us."

"Not dangerous like that," I explained. "But you might find out something bad. You might find out something you don't really want to know."

"This isn't something I just came up with. I've wanted to know this my whole life. Believe me, I'm glad they gave me up. I love my parents, but I'm incomplete. Like a book with the first chapter torn out. I need to know. . . ."

I realized there was only one answer I could give her.

"Okay. I'll do it."

"Really?" she said excitedly.

"Yes," I said. "I'll look for your parents."

"You're not going to look for them, Florian," she said. "You're going to find them."

I didn't want to make a promise I couldn't keep, but she was persuasive. "Yes. I'll find them."

There was that big smile again. The one I saw the first day we met.

"But I can't work on it today," I added. "I've got to go back to the National Gallery. I'm still trying to figure out something about the robbery."

"Okay," she said, doing a pretty bad job of masking her disappointment. "I'll see you later then."

I swallowed my last spoonful of cereal and got up to rinse

the bowl in the sink. "Why later? Aren't you coming with me to the museum?"

"I thought the FBI stuff was all top secret."

"Yeah, well, I thought you just said we were partners."

And that's where it became official. As I rinsed my bowl in the sink. Florian Bates Investigations was born.

13.

Nerds United

"SO WHY ARE WE GOING TO THE MUSEUM?" Margaret asked as we walked from the Metro station toward the National Gallery. "What are we looking for?"

"I'm not sure . . . but something," I answered, not meaning to sound so mysterious. "It just doesn't add up for me. Like the time I built the Death Star out of Legos. It looked good. Everything fit together. But I still had pieces left over. Turns out I'd skipped an entire level with a docking bay."

She flashed a smile. "Death Stars and docking bays. You really are a nerd, aren't you?"

"Nerds make the world go round," I said proudly.

"Yes, we do," she replied. "But I don't know what leftover pieces there could possibly be. We identified Novak's picture and know that he's back in the Czech Republic. All that's here are the paintings, and you already found those."

"I just think we may have missed something."

She gave me a look. "And by 'we,' you actually mean the FBI, the crime scene unit, and museum security?"

"Yeah," I said sheepishly. "That's how it goes with TOAST. You have to look for the crumbs, too."

When we entered the museum, we saw a crush of people in the rotunda and Margaret asked, "Is it my imagination, or is it more crowded than usual?"

"It's not your imagination at all," I answered. "Today's the first day they've reopened the two rooms where the pictures were stolen. Mom said attendance is expected to be high for a couple weeks. I guess everyone's suddenly interested in art."

"Either that or they think they're smarter than the FBI and can uncover some clue the experts missed," she said with a sly grin.

"Who would be crazy enough to believe that?" I replied as we both laughed.

Unfortunately, the crowds were the biggest in the rooms where we wanted to go. Our first stop was Gallery 83, which is where we saw Novak the first time, when he was asleep on the couch.

"Two paintings were stolen from here: *The Dance Class* by Edgar Degas and *Girl in White* by Vincent van Gogh," I said as I pointed to each, both now back where they belonged on each side of the door.

"And Novak was sleeping, or at least pretending to sleep, here," Margaret added as she sat down on the couch right where we saw him. I sat next to her and we scanned the room, looking at what he would have seen that day.

Margaret noticed a guard standing in the corner of the room.

"Was there a guard in here before?" she asked, motioning to the guard in the corner.

I leaned over and whispered to her, "I don't think he's actually a guard. I think he's FBI. Agent Rivers said they're going to keep a heightened presence here to see if anyone suspicious returns to the scene of the crime."

We both got a charge from the undercover feel of it all.

"But that day there wasn't anyone there?"

"Not permanently," I said. "Each guard normally rotates between three or four rooms, which is probably why Novak was here in the first place. He wanted to figure out the pattern."

"So he pretends to sleep and runs his video camera for about thirty minutes, which gives him a good sense of their schedule," she replied. "But how does he find out when the security system is going to be upgraded? Does he overhear someone talking about it?"

"No way," I said. "Information like that is kept secret. The guards probably didn't even know it was going to happen until a day or two before. My guess is that his partner found that out."

"Partner? You mean the guy who dressed up as the other custodian?"

"That would make sense," I replied. "He has to have some sort of inside connection to get the custodian's uniform. Maybe that same connection is how he found out about the security system."

"Which means it could be someone who works here at the museum," she said.

"That's a definite possibility. Somehow the thief knew they were going to reset the security system at exactly one fifteen in the morning."

"Does the FBI think there was an insider?"

"If so, they didn't share that with me," I said. "But I do know Agent Rivers is here investigating today. Maybe that's why."

"We should say hi."

"Covert asset," I reminded her. "If I see him in public, I'm supposed to act like I don't know him. You too."

I opened up a little notebook and drew a diagram of the room, making sure to mark where each picture hung and the locations of the three doorways. I wanted to have notes to refer to later at home.

"So explain this to me," she said.

"What?"

"If you're already on the inside and know when the entire security system is going to be reset, then why do you even need to have someone study the guards? And why do you go to the trouble of flying that person all the way from the Czech Republic and making him change his identity?"

"That's the part that doesn't make sense to me," I answered. "He's supposed to be an expert art thief, but you don't use him to actually steal the paintings. It's like having LeBron James on your basketball team but only having him sell hot dogs. If they just needed surveillance, I'm sure they could have found someone else. He must have had another job, something more specialized that made it worth bringing him here."

"I bet Paul and Vince know," she said.

"Who?"

"Gauguin and Van Gogh," she replied, pointing at their self-portraits in the room. "I bet they saw it all, but they're keeping it a secret just like they kept the secret of who cut off Van Gogh's ear."

I turned to look at her for a moment and said, "You're really a nerd too."

We shared a smile and it dawned on me that Margaret was the first friend I had with whom I could truly be myself. Next we went into Gallery 85, which is where we'd seen Novak painting the copy of *Woman with a Parasol* and where Renoir's *Child with Toys* was stolen. Like the first room, this one was more crowded than usual and had a guard (possibly an agent) stationed in the corner keeping an eye on things.

"And this is where he posed as a copyist," said Margaret.

"He wasn't posing," I reminded her. "He may have lied about his name, but his copy of the painting was amazing. He's supertalented. Agent Rivers says that he was a star student at the Academy of Fine Arts in Prague."

She gave me a confused look. "How does a talented artist get involved with criminals?"

"It's hard to make a living as a painter," I reasoned. "Maybe someone offered him too much money to pass up."

"Okay, then let's rephrase the question," she said.

"How does an art thief from the Czech Republic even meet someone with an inside connection to a museum in Washington?"

"That's a great question. It could be like my parents. After all, my mom's from Italy, and my dad's from Boston."

"How'd they meet?"

I smiled at the memory of a story I'd heard many times. "She was working at a small museum in Rome, and went to an international conference in London to give a speech about techniques in art conservation. My dad was at the same conference and was supposed to attend a presentation about motion detectors but walked into the wrong room by mistake. He was just about to leave when she stood up to give her talk."

"And when he saw her he decided to stay?" Margaret asked.

"Exactly," I replied. "A week later that small museum in Rome was really surprised when an American security expert offered an amazingly low price to come and consult about their new alarm system. It took him two weeks of consulting to finally work up the courage to ask her out."

Margaret laughed. "Nicely played, Mr. B. So do you think the same thing could have happened here? One of the conservators or curators or security people was in Europe going to a conference and bumped into Novak by accident? They get to know each other and instead of getting married like your parents, they decide to commit a felony."

"Maybe," I said. "But here's another question for you. Why paint *Woman with a Parasol* instead of *The Japanese Footbridge*?"

"What's *The Japanese Footbridge*?" she asked.

"That picture," I said, pointing at another painting. "It's also by Monet. If you copy it, you're facing two doorways and can see who comes and goes. But *Woman with a Parasol* is in the corner. When he painted it, he was looking away from everything."

"You're right," she said. "The other picture seems like the smarter option."

"Unless it wasn't about the room," I countered. "Maybe this was about access. The copyists keep their supplies and canvases on the same floor where my mother's studio is. It's just down the hall from the security center."

"So that lets him get downstairs where the public normally can't go," Margaret says, picking up on my train of thought. "Maybe that's when he snoops around and finds out about the security system being reset."

I thought this through for a moment.

"That's good," I said. "He goes down there every morning

to pick up all his stuff and back again in the evening to put it away. He does a little spy work along the way."

"Although it's hard to sneak around carrying a canvas and all those paints," joked Margaret.

I know she was joking, but it was a good point. And it made me think of something. "Wait a second," I said, suddenly excited. "You're absolutely right. Paintings are big and bulky."

She gave me a blank look. "I hate it when I'm right and I don't know why. It means I don't get to gloat about it."

I flashed a huge grin. "How did you know my dad borrowed his golf clubs when he was in California?"

"What?" she said, now totally confused.

"The time you figured out that my dad had played golf in California. How did you know he'd borrowed somebody else's golf clubs?"

"Because he wasn't carrying any clubs when he came home," she said. "Why is that important?"

"That's the hardest clue to find," I said. "The clue that's a clue because it's missing, not because it's there."

"And . . . ?" she asked.

"What wasn't Novak carrying at the airport?" I said, piecing it together.

"I don't know," she said. "He had a suitcase, a backpack"—

she smiled and I knew she had it—"but he didn't have the painting. He didn't have his copy of *Woman with a Parasol*. Something that beautiful that you spent eight days painting, you'd bring home with you, right?"

"I would," I said.

"Although he could have just shipped it home in the mail," she said. "I don't know if you bring something like that on a plane."

"That's true," I said. "But think about what we were just saying. He had a special talent worth bringing him all the way from Eastern Europe. What if that talent was his ability to paint? What if he didn't ship it? What if he never took it out of the museum?"

We both looked at the painting on the wall.

"You think that's his copy on the wall?" she asked.

I shrugged. "I don't know. But I think it could be."

We walked over and studied the painting, looking for any hint that it might be a forgery. I leaned forward until I was just inches from it. That's when the guard cleared his throat to get my attention.

"Back up," he said firmly.

"Sorry," I replied. "It's just beautiful, isn't it?"

"Yeah," he replied. "But it's just as beautiful from farther back."

I stepped away and he turned his attention to the rest of the room.

"What do you think?" Margaret whispered. "Is it a forgery?"

"I don't know. I'm not an art expert," I said. "Luckily I know someone who is."

I started dialing as we walked toward the elevator. I called Agent Rivers and he told us to stay in my mother's studio until all of her coworkers were gone. He wanted it to look like we were just waiting for her to finish so we could go home together. It was all part of the plan to keep my involvement hidden. The last person left around five forty-five, and a few minutes later he arrived. He'd been in the security center, so there was nothing suspicious about him being at the museum.

"Okay," he said as he locked the door to assure our privacy. "What's your big discovery?"

"It's not a discovery so much as a theory," I said, trying to lower his expectations. "But I think maybe four paintings were stolen."

Rivers and my mom shared a confused look before turning their attention to me.

"What's the fourth painting?" he asked.

"*Woman with a Parasol,*" I said.

"*Woman with a Parasol* is in Gallery Eighty-Five," Mom replied. "I saw it this morning."

"Yes, but what if it was a copy?" I suggested. "What if you saw the copy that Novak painted?"

I could see Rivers start to run the idea through his head.

"It would explain why they went to the trouble of bringing him here," Margaret added. "Studying the guards was just a side job. The main reason he was involved was so that he could paint the forgery."

All eyes turned to Margaret.

"I'm the partner," she said proudly. "We figured this part out together."

Rivers chuckled and shook his head.

"Why go to all that trouble?" Mom asked. "Why not just put it with the other paintings in the recycling?"

"It's too big," I said. "Even without the frame it wouldn't have fit in the recycling bundler."

"And you're basing this on what?" asked Rivers. "You can tell that it's a forgery?"

"No," I said. "It's just a theory."

He considered this for a moment. "Okay," he said. "Let's go have a look."

We all went up to the main floor, my mom carrying her bag like she was going home. If anyone noticed us it would just look like we were leaving for the day. We stopped in Gallery 85. Rivers made sure no one was around while my mother examined the picture closely.

"So?" he asked her. "Could it be fake?"

"If so, it's an amazingly good one," she said. "I can't tell just by looking at it. I'd have to take it down, put it under the microscope, and run some tests."

Agent Rivers thought about this for a moment and said, "No. I need you to figure it out without moving the painting."

My mother gave him a quizzical look. "Why?"

"Because we think there's an employee involved," he said.

Margaret and I shared a look and a nod.

"If it's true and if this is a copy, they think they've gotten away with it. The moment it comes off the wall, we warn them that we're on to them."

Mom considered all of this for a moment and said, "I only need a tiny flake of paint to run a cesium test."

"Brilliant," he said. "How do you order a test like that?"

"It's a lot of paperwork," she answered. "And I have to allocate the expense to a certain budget."

He shook his head. "That's way too many people involved. Get me a flake and I'll have the test run. We have labs too."

He smiled at us and nodded before walking in the opposite direction. Mom looked at the painting for a few more moments, and then we headed for the door.

"What's a cesium test?" I asked once we were outside.

"It's a way to see if a painting is old or modern," she said. "There's cesium in all the paint made after 1945 and none in the paint made before. So if you test a painting that was supposedly done in the 1800s and find any cesium in it, then . . ."

"You know it's a fake," I said.

"Exactly."

"What happened in 1945?" asked Margaret.

"That's when the first nuclear explosion took place," Mom explained. "Cesium was part of the radioactive fallout."

"And that spread everywhere?" I asked.

She nodded. "Yep. All over the world including into all the dirt and plants used for making paint."

"And that can be determined just by testing a single flake?"

"You've got to love science," she said.

Margaret shook her head and added, "Nerds really do make the world go round."

14.

The Hornet's Nest

SINCE IT WAS GOING TO TAKE A FEW DAYS TO GET the results of the cesium test, Margaret and I had time to work on our other case: the search for her birth parents. This one didn't involve any Eastern European crime syndicates or million-dollar art thefts, but I knew solving it would be just as tricky. Maybe more.

"You're sure you want to do this?" I asked as we rode the Metro.

Her answer was soft but firm. "I'm positive."

She had a determined look so I didn't suggest we play the game where we try to guess who's getting off at which stop. Instead we rode without talking much until we reached the Howard University station.

"This is our stop," I said as I stood, not that she needed to be reminded.

Even though it wasn't quite noon, the temperature was already in the nineties and rising. As we walked along the campus, the large shade trees that lined Georgia Avenue offered us a little relief from the heat.

"I understand that your adoption is a sensitive issue," I said. "But we're going to have to be able to talk about it in order for me to solve it."

"I know," she said. "What do you want to know?"

"Everything," I answered. "Tell me whatever you know."

"Not much," she replied. "On the night of August sixth somebody dropped me off at Engine House Four."

"Was it a man or a woman?" I asked.

She shrugged. "Nobody ever told me."

"Did they leave you in a crib, a stroller, or something like that?"

"The only thing I know is that I was wrapped in a blanket," she said, her eyes looking forward and not at me. "We still have it. I can show it to you later. It's yellow and has my name embroidered on it in big block letters, 'MARGARET A.'"

"A?" I said, curious. "What's the A? A middle initial? The first letter of your birth parents' last name?"

She stopped and looked at me. "I just told you everything I know. I was left at the firehouse with a blanket that said 'Margaret A' on August sixth. That's it."

"I'm sorry," I said, worrying that I had upset her. "I didn't mean to—"

"Don't be sorry," she replied. "I'm not mad that you're asking the questions. I'm just frustrated that I don't know the answers. That's why we're doing this."

"Have you talked to your parents about what they know?"

"Not much," she said. "I always worry that if I ask them anything, they'll think I'm unhappy about them being my mom and dad. And I'm not. I love them. I don't want to upset them, so I never bring it up."

"Well, we've got some solid clues to go on," I said, trying to sound positive. "Let's see where they lead us."

The firehouse was a squat two-story building made of dark brown bricks. ENG4INE was painted on one wall and there were three red barn doors for the garage. One of them was open and we could see a red-and-white fire truck inside. Written on the front of the truck was THE HORNET'S NEST.

"What's the Hornet's Nest?" asked Margaret.

I shrugged. "Let's poke it and find out."

We were heading for the office when a firefighter saw us through the open garage door.

"Are you here about CPR training?" he asked. He was young and wore dark blue pants and a matching button-up shirt with a DCFD patch on the left shoulder.

"No," I said, unsure how best to explain exactly why we were there. "We just want to find out—"

"We're looking for information," Margaret said, taking charge. "About something that happened at this station twelve years ago."

He looked us over for a moment and said, "Then you'll want to talk to the captain. He's the only one who's been here that long."

"Is he in the office?" I asked, pointing toward the door.

"No," he answered. "He's in the kitchen . . . God help us."

We followed him through the garage door and alongside the fire truck. There were hoses, lockers, and even a pole to slide down from upstairs. On the wall were rows of pictures—one taken each year of the firefighters at the station. Someone had also painted a logo of a giant hornet wearing a fire helmet and jacket holding a hose and ax. Beneath it again was written THE HORNET'S NEST.

"It's our symbol," he said, noticing me looking at it. "Don't mess with the hive."

"Cool," I answered.

The kitchen was in the back, and there a man was frying something on the stove. He was older, but fit, his blue T-shirt tight on his biceps. He had a thin white mustache and goatee.

"Twenty-six years in the department and he can still only cook three things," joked the firefighter. "What are you making today?"

"Fish sandwiches," he said. "And if you say anything more about my cooking, you're going to go without." He looked at Margaret and me and asked, "Who do we have here?"

"These two are looking for information about something that happened here twelve years ago," he said. "I told them they needed to talk to someone old like you."

He flipped a pair of fish patties with a spatula, causing a sudden sizzle.

"What could you two possibly want to know about from twelve years ago?" he asked. "Were you even born yet?"

"I was," said Margaret. "About a week earlier. That's why I'm here."

There was something about what she said and the way she said it that caught his attention. He looked at her more intently, and slowly a smile came over his face. "Are you her? What was her name again? Mary? Mallory?"

"Margaret," she said.

"That's it!" he replied, his face lighting up. "You're Margaret, aren't you?"

"You remember me?" she asked, small tears suddenly welling up in her eyes.

"I don't remember *you*," he said with a laugh. "I remember a baby about this big." He held up his hands like he was cupping a small baby. "Look how much you've grown."

They stood there frozen by the moment. Everything about it was perfect. Except for the smell.

"Cap," said the firefighter. "Cap. Your fish. It's burning!"

The captain snapped out of it and looked down at the pan, a plume of dark smoke suddenly rising from the patties.

"Well, you're a firefighter," he said. "Do something about it. I'm going to talk to my old friend."

He handed the younger man the spatula and walked over to Margaret. The two of them looked at each other for a moment, and he introduced himself.

"Captain Joseph Abraham, DC Fire Department," he said.

"Margaret Campbell," she replied. "It's a pleasure to meet you."

"The pleasure is all mine." They shook hands, and he

never broke eye contact and never stopped smiling. "What can I do for you?"

"I want to find out where I come from," she said. "I want to find out who my parents are."

His smile suddenly disappeared. "I'm not so sure that's a good idea. And even if it was, I don't know that I could help you."

"Can you at least tell me about that night?" she asked hopefully. "I was here in the firehouse until the next morning, right?"

He thought about this for a second and nodded. "You were. I can tell you about that."

Margaret flashed a huge grin. The captain went to say something else, but then he turned and looked at me as though it was the first time he'd noticed I was there.

"Who's this?" he asked her.

"My best friend," she answered.

"Florian," I said.

"Nice to meet you, Florian," he replied. "Why don't you two come with me?"

He led us upstairs. Most of the second story was the dormitory where everyone sleeps, but there were two big rooms, one marked LOUNGE that had a big-screen TV and seven matching recliners, and one marked LIBRARY that had a pair of couches and a bookcase. That's where he took us.

"Have a seat," he said, motioning to one couch while he sat down on the other.

"So you were actually here that night?" Margaret asked. "The night I was"—she paused for a moment looking for the right word—"left."

"Yes, I was," he replied.

"What can you remember about it?"

"It was summer, about this time, right?"

"Right," she said. "August sixth."

"Most of us were in the TV room watching a baseball game—I don't remember who was playing—and the bell rang. The doorbell, not the fire alarm. So we sent a probie to answer it."

"What's a probie?" I asked.

"A probationary firefighter," he said. "A trainee. Probies usually get stuck with all the errands. His name was Munson, Tom Munson. So he goes down there and we keep expecting him to come back, but he doesn't. Eventually the inning ends and a couple of us go downstairs to see what's what. Imagine our surprise when we find Tom holding a baby and talking to a young man, African-American, around twenty years old."

"Was it my father?" asked Margaret anxiously.

"I don't think so. But you have to realize the sanctuary

law is designed to protect the baby. And one of the ways the law protects the baby is that it doesn't allow us to ask questions. The firehouse is a safe haven, and if you can't take care of your baby, you can bring her here without getting in trouble. So we didn't ask him if he was your father. That said, I think he mentioned something about being a friend of your mother's."

All of this was new information to Margaret, and I could tell it was a little overwhelming.

"Do you remember anything about him?" I asked.

"Not really," he answered. "It was late and I was only down there with him for about a minute. But, like I said, our concern wasn't him, it was her."

He looked right at Margaret and smiled.

"You know this is where you slept that night?" he added.

"Here?" she said, looking around the library.

"Yeah, we took turns all night long," he told her. "Let me show you something."

Two bookshelves were filled with photo albums. He went over, picked one out, and started flipping through it. The pages were filled with images ranging from firefighters in action to goofy shots around the firehouse. He stopped when he found what he was looking for and turned the book around so that we could see it.

"That's you that night," he said.

He pointed to a picture of a baby wrapped in a yellow blanket being held by one firefighter and surrounded by another five. He peeled back the plastic cover, took the picture out of the album, and handed it to Margaret.

"Tom Munson is the one holding you; he's the probie who answered the door," he said.

"And is this you?" Margaret asked, pointing at a younger version of the man sitting across from us.

"Yes, it is. It's funny because back then you were the one who was bald and I was the one who had hair. That's all changed now."

She looked at the blanket and read the embroidery out loud. "MARGARET A."

"I wish we knew what the A stood for," I said.

Captain Abraham smiled. "We decided it stood for Angel. That's what we called you, Margaret Angel."

15.

Not a Buffalo

WE STAYED AND TALKED TO CAPTAIN ABRAHAM for another fifteen minutes, but most of the conversation was Margaret filling him in on her life. It was as if she'd discovered a long-lost uncle who wanted to know about everything from soccer to school. He was excited to hear her team was playing for the city championship and said that Deal was one of the best schools in the District. I just sat back and kept my mouth shut, trying to stay out of the way of the conversation but making sure to pay attention for anything that might help us find her birth parents. With regard to potential clues, we were left with two:

1. The names of everyone who was on duty that night.

2. A copy of the photo of Margaret with all the firefighters. This one was a little tricky because Abraham didn't want to let us take it for fear that the original might never come back. He promised to have a copy made and send it to her, but just to be safe, when he got up to introduce her to one of his coworkers, I secretly snapped a picture of it with my phone.

When it was time to leave, he gave her an Engine 4 shoulder patch with the Hornet's Nest logo. He also gave her some advice: "Don't look any further than this," he warned. "I know you think you want to know who your birth parents are, and that's understandable. But your life started here, that night, when Tom took you in his arms. That's when you were born. There's no need to look any earlier than that."

Whether or not she intended to follow this advice, she respected him enough to say, "I'll think about it."

I could tell he was about to make another argument, but

instead he stopped himself and said, "Don't forget to give me your address, so I can send you a copy of that picture."

He pulled a business card out of his wallet and turned it over so that she could write it on the back.

"And stop by for lunch sometime," he added.

"Let me guess," she replied. "You'll make fish sandwiches."

He laughed. "I promise not to burn yours."

He walked us to the door, and just as we were about to leave, he leaned over and whispered into my ear, "You take care of our girl, okay?"

I looked back at him and nodded. "Yes, sir. I'll do whatever it takes."

He winked and replied, "Good answer."

Margaret and I walked for nearly a block before either of us said a word. I wanted to give her a chance to think through everything that'd just happened. Finally she simply said, "Wow."

"You're not kidding," I replied. "I was completely wrong about coming here. I thought it was a bad idea, but that was awesome."

"It's weird because I've always known this story," she said. "But now, seeing the place, talking to someone who was there, for the first time it seems real."

"I'm guessing your promise to 'think about it' doesn't include you actually thinking about it," I added.

"No way," she replied. "I still want to keep looking. I'm more determined than ever."

"That's what I figured," I said.

We were walking alongside the Howard University campus again and I pulled my phone out of my pocket. "I've got a little surprise for you," I told her as I opened it to the picture of Margaret with the firefighters.

"Sneaky," she said as she took the phone. "When'd you get this?"

"When he introduced you to the paramedic," I said. "It's just a picture of a picture, so the quality's not great. But it should do until he sends you a better one."

"Thanks. It's a great picture, isn't it?"

"Actually, it's even better than you think."

"What do you mean?"

I zoomed in past the firefighters so that only the image of Margaret filled the screen.

"What do you see?" I asked.

"A baby . . . in a blanket . . . surrounded by firefighters," she answered, unsure what I was getting at.

"And what's the baby wearing?"

She looked at the picture more closely. Even though the

blanket covered most of her, you could still make out a little bit of what she was wearing.

"Looks like a onesie," she said. "With a little buffalo on it."

"That's not a buffalo," I replied. "Technically it's a bison."

She rolled her eyes. "Okay, so *technically* it's a bison. Why is that important?"

I looked up to draw her attention to the banners that hung from the streetlight we were standing near. They matched the ones on all the streetlights along Georgia Avenue. On one side was a picture of a Howard University student. On the other it said I BLEED BISON BLUE!

"The name of the team at Howard is the Bison," she said, putting it together.

"Yep," I replied. "And judging by this onesie, I wouldn't be surprised if you were born at Howard University Hospital."

Her eyes lit up. "That's a-mazing," she said, dragging out the word. "I can't believe I missed that."

"Well, you had a lot going on. That's why you hired me, remember?"

"Let's go to the hospital and look at the records from the week I was born," she said excitedly. "We can find the answer right now."

"It's not that easy," I told her. "They won't just show you

hospital records. There are privacy issues involved."

Her elation turned to frustration.

"But we can go over there and look around," I suggested. "You said that just being at the firehouse helped. Maybe visiting the hospital will help too."

The hospital was on the other side of the campus. It was nine stories tall and a couple blocks wide. According to the directory, Labor and Delivery was on the third floor. While we waited for the elevator, Margaret grabbed a brochure from an information stand in the lobby.

"'Howard University Hospital was founded in 1862 to care for freed slaves,'" she said, reading from it. "'It was originally called the Freedmen's Hospital.'"

"A hospital with history," I said. "How cool is that?"

"Yeah," she replied as we stepped onto the elevator. "The question is, am I part of that history?"

On the third floor we made it only as far as the waiting room. You have to be the family member of a patient to get beyond that. Still, we found something interesting. On one wall of the waiting room was a giant collage made up of pictures of babies who'd been born at the hospital. In some of the older-looking pictures, many of the babies were wearing the exact same onesie that Margaret had on in her picture from the firehouse.

"Look," she said, pointing at it. "It's identical. This is the place."

"That's how TOAST works," I reminded her. "One little detail at a time."

After the hospital, we went back to my house and I dug some leftover Chinese food out of the fridge for lunch. "You want chicken lo mein? Or beef and broccoli?" I asked, holding up both cartons.

"I'm not much of a broccoli girl," she said as she took the lo mein. "Got any leftover egg rolls?"

"Never," I said with a satisfied smile on my face. "I always finish off the egg rolls. It's too risky to leave them for later."

"Risky how?"

"Three reasons: One, my dad could eat them; two, the electricity could go out and they could spoil in the refrigerator; and three, in the event of the zombie apocalypse they would remain uneaten for all eternity. Total tragedy."

"Clearly you've thought this through."

"That's the kind of thoroughness you can expect from Florian Bates Investigations," I said. "So, why don't we work on the case?"

Inspired by what we'd seen at FBI Headquarters, we made a case board using an old corkboard the previous owners of the house had left in the basement. I printed a copy of the picture of Margaret and the firefighters and pinned it in the middle. We also put up the list of the firefighters who were on duty that night and the brochure from Howard University Hospital.

"Before we continue, there's something I've been trying to figure out," I said.

"What?"

"Do you think we should give our cases numbers or names?"

"That's what you think is important?" she asked, incredulous.

"You're the one who wanted to start the New FBI," I reminded her. "We have to figure out everything. Even stupid little organizational details. And nothing helps organization more than consistency. So is this case one? Or do we give it a name?"

"We should definitely give it a name," she said. "Numbers will be hard to remember later, but names will stick out."

"I couldn't agree more. So what do we call this one?"

She took a bite of lo mein while she thought about it. "How about Hornet's Nest?"

"I like it," I said. "It's much better than the name I was thinking of."

"What name did you have?" she asked.

"The case of Finding Out Who Margaret's Birth Parents Are," I replied.

"Very clever."

"Clever is what I was going for," I joked.

She took the shoulder patch with the Hornet's Nest logo and stuck it to the top of the case board.

"Now it's official."

We went online and tried to track down the other firefighters who were on duty the night Margaret was left at Engine House Four. Their names were:

Tom Munson

Vince Jackson

Jerry Cavanaugh

Bill Baker

John Reynolds

Unfortunately, these were very normal names. It's a lot easier to find people with unusual ones like Philo T. Farnsworth (who invented the television) or Bronko Nagurski (who was one of the first-ever football stars). It turned out there were seventeen different Vincent Jacksons living in Washington and eleven Bill Bakers. Finding the right ones was going to take time. However, we did get lucky with Jerry Cavanaugh.

On the website for the DC Fire Department, we found a link to the Emerald Society, a fraternal organization made up of local firefighters of Irish descent. It's a social group that raises money for charities, and on one of their pages, we found a picture of Jerry Cavanaugh marching in the St. Patrick's Day parade. He was wearing an emerald-green beret and had a thick mustache. Even though he was older and his mustache had grayed, it was easy to recognize him from the picture we already had.

"It says he's a captain with Engine Company Twenty-One," Margaret said. "We should call."

"Nobody's stopping you," I told her.

She flashed a nervous smile and dialed the number. It turned out he was off duty, but it was still a step in the right direction. She wrote "Engine Co. 21" by his name on the case board.

The least common name on the list also turned out to be the most frustrating. None of the Tom Munsons we found in the DC area had any connection to the fire department. After the seventh one, Margaret stood up and stretched.

"You want to call it a day and start up again tomorrow?" she asked.

"I can't tomorrow," I said. "I got a text from Agent Rivers. I've got training."

"What type?"

I shrugged. "FBI training, I guess."

"Well, we'll get to it soon," she said. "Thanks for today."

"My pleasure," I replied. "And we're going to find them. You know why?"

"Why?"

"Because Florian Bates Investigations uncovers the mysteries of the world, one case at a time."

She smiled. "You see? It's catchy."

16.
Quantico

AGENT RIVERS PICKED ME UP AT PRECISELY seven fifteen in the morning, just like he said he would. This time there was no black, armored-plated SUV with bullet-proof windows. Instead he drove a maroon hybrid with a parking permit for the Harvard Club of Washington, DC. So, while we didn't have any extra protection from random gunfire, we were well prepared should an emergency philosophy discussion break out. His usual uniform of dark suit and matching tie had been replaced by sweatpants and a T-shirt, both neatly ironed and bearing the shield of the FBI.

"Ready for your big day?" he asked as we merged into the traffic heading south on the interstate.

"As ready as I can be considering I don't really know what I'm doing," I replied. Beyond the pickup time and the instruction to bring gym clothes, the text was pretty vague on details.

"It's just some introductory training," he replied. "If you're going to be a consultant with the Bureau, you'll need to do this every now and then. It's what we call a necessary evil."

"And we're training together?"

"No. I have to take a couple recertification courses," he said. "I'd already scheduled them about a month ago and figured we might as well take care of yours at the same time. And this way your parents don't have to drive you down to Quantico and wait in the lobby all day."

Quantico is a Marine Corps base in rural Virginia that's home to the FBI training center. It took us about an hour and a half to get there, and during that time I learned the following things about Agent Rivers:

1. Although his car was almost as clean as his office, a pair of empty cups in the cup holders indicated he's a fan of gourmet coffee.

2. Unlike the agent who drove us in the SUV, he never goes so much as one mile over the speed limit.

3. Judging by his reactions to sports talk radio, he's an avid fan of the Washington Nationals baseball team.

4. When I asked him about a trumpet case in the backseat, he told me he plays in a band called Funk Brothers Incorporated that performs at Bureau parties and weddings and is made up entirely of fellow agents.

We got off the interstate at a town named Garrisonville, and I started to get a little . . . I don't know if "anxious" is the right word, but I was definitely curious about the day ahead.

"Can you tell me what kind of training it is?" I asked. "Or is it top secret?"

"It's not a secret from you," he said. "Your schedule is sticking out of the briefcase behind my seat."

I reached back and grabbed the paper.

As I read it, my mood turned to instant excitement. "Are you serious?" I exclaimed. "This is going to be epic. We're talking the best day of my life."

"See, I told you," he answered.

"Tactical and evasive driving. Weapons training. Explosives!" I shook my head in amazement. "Explosives?!"

"Oops," he said. "That sounds like *my* schedule. Yours must be the other sheet."

I reached back and grabbed another piece of paper, and when I saw it I came straight back to reality. "Classroom study. Self-defense. Hostage preparedness."

"That sounds more like it," he said.

"Don't you mean that sounds more boring?" I replied.

"Trust me," he said. "It may not be the most exciting day of your life, but it'll be more fun than you think. Besides, you'll probably be able to hear the explosives go off, and the boom is half the fun."

"Who's Johan Blankvort of Bethesda, Maryland?" I asked, reading the name off the top of the schedule.

"You are," he said. "Which reminds me. There's a present for you in the glove compartment."

I opened it but didn't see anything presentlike. "What am I looking for?" I asked.

"The wallet," he said.

"You're giving me money?" I asked, confused.

"No, the wallet is the present," he said. "It's one of those recycled deals. They're very hip right now."

Normally, when adults say something's hip, it definitely isn't. But the wallet was kind of cool. Inside there was a student ID from North Bethesda Middle School, a Montgomery

County library card, and a summer YMCA pool pass, all made in the name of Johan Blankvort, but with my picture. There was also a Scooper-Star loyalty club card from the Wow Cow ice cream shop.

"Am I going undercover?" I asked.

"Kind of," he said. "But not like you think. You're only lying to the rest of the FBI. We don't want the name Florian Bates to appear anywhere in the Bureau's records. For you to be a true covert asset, we need to fully protect your identity."

"Then how do we explain why Johan Blankvort is getting a day of FBI training? Won't people find that suspicious?"

"He—I mean you—won an essay contest about 'What America Means to Me.' This is first prize."

"Nice," I said. "I hope my essay was good."

"Moved me to tears," he replied with a laugh. "You should be very proud. Also, one more cone at Wow Cow and your next one's free. So you've got that going for you."

I'd never been on a military base before and it took a bit to get used to the Marines carrying guns, but the training center had its own little section and looked like a small college. I checked in, as Johan Blankvort, and was told to go to Gymnasium 4. Rivers had time before his first class so he showed me the way.

There were already several training sessions under way once we got to the gym, and it didn't take a detective to notice what the instructors had in common. Each looked like he belonged in a mixed-martial-arts cage match.

Except for mine.

My instructor looked like she taught kindergarten. She was barely five feet tall, had her hair pulled back in a ponytail, and wore knee-length black workout pants and a gray T-shirt with FBI written in big black letters across the chest. She was doing some stretches and smiled when she saw us.

Agent Rivers talked to her off to the side so no one could hear what they were saying. Judging by her expression and the way he put his hand on her shoulder, I got the impression they knew each other well. Once they were done, he took care of the introductions.

"I'd like you to meet Agent Cross," he said.

"Just call me Kayla," she added, offering her hand.

"Nice to meet you, Kayla," I answered as we shook. "I'm . . . Johan."

They laughed. "Actually, Kayla's the one person here today who knows who you really are. But that's good. Keep it up," said Agent Rivers. Then he turned to her and added, "I told you he was sharp."

"Good to know," she said. "Come on, Johan. Let's see how sharp you are on the mat."

I already felt self-conscious because of my age and the elementary-school feel of my instructor. But then we started doing yoga poses and it became downright ridiculous. I noticed guys smirking as they did their push-ups nearby.

"Ignore them," she said, reading my reaction. "Training tip number one: Do your thing and don't worry about what anyone else thinks. You only need to worry about you."

I nodded. "Got it."

"Now here's the scenario," she said once we were limbered up. "I'm the victim and you're the perp. That's what we call the bad guy. I'm walking home all alone on a dark street and you attack me. Show me how you do it?"

My specific memory of what happened next is sketchy. I do recall approaching her from behind and trying to wrap my arms around her. There was an iron grip around my wrist and a high-pitched scream. I'm pretty sure the scream was me. (Okay, I'm positive the scream was me.) Then I remember flying through the air upside down. When I landed on the mat, the image that ran through my head was that of my mother slamming dough against the counter when she makes homemade pizza.

"Unfff," I said as the air rushed out of my body. It took

me a second to catch my breath, and when I opened my eyes I saw Agent Rivers. He'd leaned over to look at me, and from my point of view he was upside down.

"Oh, by the way, don't let her appearance fool you," he said. "She's kinda like a ninja."

He cackled and walked away promising, "I'll pick you up at four. Try to stay in one piece."

Kayla was my instructor for the entire day and somehow maintained her cheery disposition, no matter what we were doing. We spent another hour and a half practicing self-defense, and my biggest accomplishment was that I went the last twenty-five minutes of that exercise without going airborne. The classroom session was all about standard FBI protocols and procedures, and while it was beyond boring, my aching body needed the rest. Lunch was in a massive cafeteria called a "mess." I had a sub sandwich and chips. She had quinoa salad and a bowl of soup.

"Let me guess," I said halfway through the meal. "You're a vegetarian and you grew up in Philadelphia."

She smiled. "That's right. How'd you know? I still have the accent?"

"Not really," I answered. "But you called my sandwich a hoagie, and that's a total Philly thing."

"And you guessed vegetarian because it was the only way

to explain why I'd pass up everything else for quinoa and vegetable soup?"

I nodded. "Pretty much."

"You're good, Johan Blankvort," she joked. "Very, very good."

Hostage preparedness class involved a lot of role-playing scenarios. Each one had an exotic name like Tokyo Takeaway or Stockholm Surprise. Kayla would put me in a situation—such as tying my hands behind my back and placing a hood over my head—and ask me what I should do next. I'll admit that I didn't pay as much attention as I should have, but at the time, getting kidnapped seemed about as likely as going to the moon. (I know, crazy stupid.)

Our final session was my favorite. We went to Hogan's Alley, which is a fake town located on the base. It has houses, a diner, a post office, and other small businesses, and it's populated by real people, except they're actors. You're supposed to interact with them like you're an FBI agent.

The exercise was a team competition. Kayla and I were paired as partners and put up against two cadets from the academy. I don't know for sure if they were smirking during yoga, but they totally seemed like the type.

A senior agent was in charge and explained the situation. "The Bank of Hogan has just been robbed. You two are the lead team," he said, pointing at the others. "And you two are support," he said, pointing at us. "I want you to go inside, inspect the scene, and question witnesses. You've only got ten minutes. When the time is up, you need to give me a full rundown of what the next steps should be."

Before we started, Kayla pulled me to the side for a little pep talk. "The key to any team is knowing its greatest strength. What's ours?"

I thought about it for a second. "The fact that these two guys don't think there's a chance in the world that a woman and a kid can beat them."

She flashed a devious grin. "That's exactly right. And what are we going to do?"

"Destroy them."

"I like you more and more all the time, Johan Blankvort."

We entered the bank, and the two other agents instantly took charge. Just by the way they talked it was obvious they'd seen way too many cop movies and pictured themselves as action heroes. Every now and then Kayla and I shared a conspiratorial smirk and shook our heads.

Still, we had to work together, so we took statements and did our best to establish the facts of the robbery. The eyewitnesses all told the same basic story with each providing a unique detail or two.

Here's what they said:

Two men wearing masks entered the bank with shotguns drawn. They forced all the employees and customers into the vault and locked them inside while they raided the cash drawers. One of the customers saw the robbers getting out of a dark blue pickup truck. A teller noticed that one of them had a star tattooed on the back of his hand. And the bank manager said that, when they left, they sped away south on Oak Street, which is the direction of the train station.

When our time was up, the agent in charge instructed us all to stop.

"It took five minutes for the victims to get released from the vault, five minutes for the FBI to arrive, and ten minutes for you to examine the scene," he said. "That means your perps have at least a twenty-minute head start and time is at a premium. What do you do next?"

As the lead detectives, the cadets went first, still in full Hollywood mode.

"Roadblocks are pointless; they've had too much of a head start," said one. "Still, we need to put out a BOLO." He stopped, looked straight at me, and smugly added, "That means 'Be on the lookout.'" Then he turned to the others and resumed. "For a blue pickup truck and a man with a star tattoo on the back of his hand. We should access security footage from any businesses along this road and reach out to our friends in the armed forces because there's a good chance these two are ex-military."

"Why do you say that?" asked the man in charge.

"Gut feeling, sir."

"On top of that," added the other, "a train left the station at three twenty-seven. We should stop it and perform a hard target search of each car in case they ditched the truck and are taking the train to some sort of rendezvous point."

"How do you know there was a train at three twenty-seven?" asked the agent in charge.

The cadet smiled, proud of this discovery. "There's a schedule on the counter. I checked it as soon as I heard what direction they'd headed."

"Very impressive," said the agent in charge. "And you both agree with this course of action?"

They nodded with supreme confidence.

"What about you two?" he asked Kayla and me.

We shared a look, and I could tell by her expression that we'd both come up with the same solution.

"Go ahead," she said to me. "You tell him."

"Well, that all sounds very good and official," I said, referring to the other agents' response. "Especially that BOLO thing. But I think it would require a lot of manpower and resources."

"You can't cut corners when it comes to a bank robbery," one of them said to me.

"All that matters is putting cuffs on the bad guy," said the other.

"That's what I figured," I replied. "So shouldn't we just arrest the bank manager?"

Kayla and the agent in charge both started laughing, and the two cadets just looked at me like I was speaking some foreign language.

"If he was locked in the vault with everybody else, then he couldn't have seen which direction they drove off," I explained. "Unless he's part of the team and trying to send us chasing the wrong leads. I say we arrest him and put the pressure on him to give up his partners."

"How old are you, son?" asked the agent in charge.

"Twelve and a half, sir," I replied.

"Great job," he said. "I'm pretty sure we'll all be working for you one day." Then he stopped and looked at the other two. "Well, maybe not all of us."

I kind of felt bad for the other two, but Kayla was in heaven as we walked back to the main complex. When we were halfway there we met up with Agent Rivers, who was returning from explosives class.

"It was bee-yoou-ti-ful," she told him. "These two

Hollywood guys are running around all macho, and then Florian solves the case in a second. I think they're still sitting there with their mouths open trying to figure out what just happened."

Agent Rivers smiled, a hint of pride on his face.

"I told you," he said to her.

"You sure did," she replied.

"Nicely done, Florian," he said. "So what did you think about your day at the FBI Academy?"

"I liked it. A lot," I said. "Except for the part about being thrown through the air. That hurt. But I liked the rest."

"And Kayla?"

"Kayla's the best," I said. Then I looked at him for a moment and decided to show off a little. "Of course, you already know that, considering she's your girlfriend."

They both stopped walking and gave me a dumbfounded look. I basked in the moment without saying much. It really is my favorite part of solving a mystery—the instant you get to share what you've figured out and everybody else gives you that look.

"H-How did . . . ?" he stammered.

"What?" I asked. "Was I not supposed to know?"

17.

The Trouble with Secrets

AS WE WALKED TOWARD THE MAIN COMPLEX from Hogan's Alley, I had a bounce in my step. Not only had I done well in the bank robbery exercise, but I'd also figured out that Agent Rivers and Kayla were boyfriend and girlfriend.

"How did you know that?" asked Rivers.

I smiled broadly and began to reconstruct.

"Well, there were about four clues in all," I said. "The first was when I got in the car. I'm not exactly tall, but even I had to move the seat back. That means the person who normally sits in that seat is shorter than I am."

I looked over at Kayla, who stood no more than five feet tall.

"Then I saw the way you talked to her when we first arrived," I said. "You put your hand on her shoulder and she lit up when she saw you. I could tell you were friends. Maybe even good friends."

"See what I mean?" Rivers said to her. "He sees everything."

"It's good," she replied. "But it's not enough. Like you said, we might just be friends. What are the other clues?"

"The biggest one was your name," I explained.

"How was my name a clue?" she wondered.

"There were two coffee cups in Agent Rivers's car," I said. "One had 'Marcus' written on it and the other . . ."

". . . had 'Kayla.'"

"But that wasn't even the clincher," I added.

"No?" she asked, smiling, playing along for my benefit. "What was the clincher?"

Before I could answer, Agent Rivers interrupted and said, "The nail polish."

Now I was the one caught off guard.

"That's right," I said, confused. "There was a small bottle of nail polish in the glove compartment. It's the same color you're wearing now." I turned to Agent Rivers, surprised that he had figured this out. "How did you know I'd seen it?"

"Well, that's the reason I put it there in the first place," he said. "And the reason I had you look for your wallet in my glove compartment. I wanted you to see it."

Now I was totally confused. "I don't understand. Why?"

"It's part of your training, Florian. Maybe the most important part. The truth is, Kayla's not my girlfriend. I planted those clues to see if you would put them together. You're clever, so I had to make them obscure. But I knew you couldn't resist snapping the pieces together."

"Oh," I said, embarrassed. "You were trying to make fun of me?"

"No, no, no," he said. "I would never do that. Florian, I am totally in awe of you. You have a once-in-a-generation gift. There aren't three agents in the Bureau who would have put all of that together."

I was still confused by it all. "How was that part of my training?"

"It was a test to see if you could be led in a direction. It's one reason why it's so important we keep your identity secret. No one will ever see you coming, which makes your talent that much more valuable. But if anyone knows you're working for us, they can set traps for you. Just like I did. They can misdirect you."

I didn't know how to respond. I couldn't believe I'd fallen for it.

"I still say it's incredible," added Kayla. "Absolutely incredible."

She put her finger under my chin and lifted it up so that I looked up from the ground. "It was a total pleasure, Florian."

"Thank you," I said, trying to shake my suddenly sour mood. "I really appreciate your help."

She smiled and stared into my eyes until I finally smiled back. Then she turned to Rivers. "It was fun being your pretend girlfriend for a day. You know, if you wanted, you could always ask me out on a date and we could see what it would be like without the pretend part."

I couldn't tell how serious she was, but it was the first time I'd seen Rivers flustered.

"I'll put that under advisement," he said.

She gave him a hug and headed toward the locker room.

Rivers and I continued walking.

"I'm really sorry, Florian."

"About what?" I asked.

"About setting you up," he said. "It didn't really turn out like I meant. To be honest, I began to think you couldn't put it together because it was too hard. And when you did, I didn't consider how it'd make you feel."

"No, it's a good lesson for me," I replied. "Are we going home now?"

"Not yet," he said. "We still have to stop by the lab."

The FBI lab was located on the edge of the campus. Rivers flashed a badge to get us past two security points, and we took an elevator to the fifth floor.

"What's up here?" I asked.

"Ancillary field equipment and devices."

I gave him a raised-eyebrow look. "You guys really hate English, don't you?"

"Gadgets," he said with a laugh. "Very cool gadgets."

This was where I got my panic button disguised as an asthma inhaler as well as a pair of sunglasses that had a small camera built into the frames.

"What do I need that for?" I asked him.

"You don't," he said. "But they're cool and I thought you might like them."

I smiled. "That works for me."

"I also want you to have this SmarTrip card," he said. "It's good to ride on any Metro or bus in and around the District."

"I've already got one," I said. "I use it all the time."

"Well, this one's a little different," he said. "First of all, you never have to put any money on it. It resets automatically, so you ride free forever."

"Cool," I said.

"Even cooler is the chip that's in it. We can track wherever it goes. Like those chips you put into a dog collar in case your dog gets away."

"Isn't that what the panic button's for?" I asked.

"No," he said. "You press the panic button when you're having trouble. If you do, we come crashing through the door, so your cover's blown. This just lets us keep track of where you are."

"Okay," I said. "I guess that's a good thing."

"Don't worry, we're not going to spy on you," he assured me. "We just want you to be safe. Now let's go down to the basement to see a friend."

We rode the elevator to sublevel four and walked against the tide of people leaving for the day until we reached a door.

"Who's the friend?" I asked.

"His name is Dr. Eduardo Gonzalez and he's one of the world's preeminent forensic scientists." He went to open the door but stopped right as his hand reached the handle and turned to me. "He's also a little . . . strange . . . but in a good way."

We stepped into a room filled with the sound of Spanish music and where numbers were scribbled all over the walls. I got the impression the doctor didn't waste time looking for paper when an idea struck. Experiments appeared to be under way on three different tables, and he was working on the one in the middle. He had wild curly hair and sang along with the music. What he lacked in vocal ability he more than made up for in volume. He was so focused on the experiment (and the music) that it took him about twenty seconds to notice us.

"Old Man Rivers," he said, looking up from his microscope. "Qué pasa?"

"Not much. How you doing, Gonzo?"

The scientist's happy mood disappeared the instant he noticed that I was in the room too.

"Who's this?"

"A friend," said Agent Rivers. "Johan Blankvort."

"*Buenas tardes,*" I said, trying to win him over.

"*Buenas tardes,*" he said skeptically.

"He's the one whose grandmother I told you about," Rivers said to him.

I had absolutely no idea what he was talking about, and reading my confusion, Rivers turned to me and explained.

"I told him that your grandmother found a painting in her attic and didn't know if it was an antique or a fake," he said to me. "I hope you don't mind."

"No," I said, still unsure what was going on.

"You see, I wanted Gonzo here to run a test to tell us if

the paint was old or new. That way we'll know what we've got on our hands."

I finally realized that this was what he'd done with the paint chip from *Woman with a Parasol*.

"Except I told him I'm not supposed to use the equipment for unauthorized jobs," Gonzalez said. "A test like that costs the taxpayers."

Now I realized that this was also a negotiation.

"How much did it cost the taxpayers?" asked Rivers. "Box seats for the Nationals game?" He pulled a pair of tickets out of his pocket and put them on the table. Gonzalez didn't pick up the tickets, but he did look at them.

"Yankees game, Sunday afternoon," he said admiringly. "That might cover the cost of the test. But when you dropped off the paint chip, you also said you wanted the job rushed. The rush costs extra."

"I thought it might," said Rivers. "That's why I brought another pair for the following Sunday."

He laid another pair of tickets on the table. Gonzalez scooped them up and slipped them into the pocket of his lab coat. "Let me see if the results are in."

When the scientist ducked into a little office, Rivers turned to me and whispered, "He doesn't even use the tickets for himself. He gives them to the Boys and Girls Club.

He likes to act like he's tough, but he's one of the good guys."

Two minutes later, Gonzalez came back with a printout and handed it to Rivers, who looked at it with total confusion.

"You know, of the three people in this room, only one of us is actually a nuclear scientist," he said. "You mind translating?"

Gonzalez pointed at some of the numbers on the printout. "See that? It's strontium." He pointed to another and added, "And that's cesium."

"What does that mean?" I asked.

He looked at me over the top of his glasses and said, "It means your grandmother's picture is no antique. It was definitely painted after 1945."

Rivers and I shared a look. The *Woman with a Parasol* hanging in the museum was a fake.

18.

The Dinner Party

THAT NIGHT MY PARENTS HELD A HASTILY arranged dinner party at our house. Since the get-together was his idea, Agent Rivers wanted to buy and bring the food, but Mom refused, insisting that cooking for six was no trouble.

"All I have to do is double the ingredients of what I was already going to make," she explained. "Besides, anyone who knows me knows I always cook for the guests in my house. If we brought food in, people would instantly suspect we were up to something. And we don't want that, do we?"

"No, we don't," agreed Agent Rivers.

(Of course that's because they were definitely up to something.)

He'd come up with his plan on the way back from Quantico and spent most of the drive on the phone with my parents and his boss. He wanted to meet with a small team that he could trust and needed to do it away from the Bureau and the National Gallery. Right now the only other people who knew the Monet hanging in the museum was a fake were the people responsible for taking it. He didn't want to do anything that might attract attention or indicate that there'd been a development in the case. So rather than meet around a conference table at the Hoover Building, everyone sat around the kitchen table at our house.

The other guests were Serena Miller, director of security at the National Gallery, and Oliver Hobbes, the representative from the insurance company. Luckily, both lived near us, so they were able to come on short notice. They were under the impression it was a social gathering until we were about half way through my mom's chicken risotto. That's when Agent Rivers stepped into another room to take a phone call.

"Sorry for the interruption," he said when he returned. "But there are some important things we have to discuss and I had to wait for approval before I could move forward."

"Does that mean there are new developments in the case?" asked Hobbes.

"You could say that," answered Rivers. He hesitated for a moment before dropping the bombshell. "A fourth painting has been stolen."

There was silence around the table as they waited to see if this was some sort of joke. Even my parents, who'd already heard the news, looked shocked all over again.

"You can't be serious," gasped Hobbes.

"I'm sorry to say that I am."

"Then what are we doing here?" asked Miller urgently. "We need to get to the museum."

"No, we don't," said the agent, making a calming motion with his hands. "That's why I asked Francesca and Jim to invite you here. *This* is where we need to be. This is where we need to develop our strategy."

"When did this even happen?" asked Miller.

"It was stolen the same night as the others," he said. "Except, unlike them, this one was swapped with a forgery."

"Which painting?" Hobbes asked.

"*Woman with a Parasol,*" answered Rivers.

Hobbes and Miller looked like they were going to faint. "That's one of the signature pieces in the entire collection," he said. "It's irreplaceable."

"I know," replied Rivers. "Which is why we're going to get it back."

He went step-by-step through everything he knew, careful to speak only in facts, not theories. He minimized my role in the discovery of the fraud, because although we were all on the same side, as far as Hobbes and Miller knew, my involvement was limited to the night of the burglary. They weren't supposed to find out about my relationship with the FBI. In fact, that's one of the reasons we had the meeting at our house. It gave me a good excuse to be there. I was in listening mode, not speaking up.

"Now comes the tricky part," said the agent as the others looked through the report from Dr. Gonzalez. "We're going to keep it a secret from everybody who's not in this room. We're all going to act like the painting on display in Gallery Eighty-Five is the masterpiece by Monet."

"That's unacceptable," exclaimed Miller. "I'm the museum's director of security and have a responsibility to my board of trustees and executive officers. If one of the most important paintings in our collection has been stolen, I have to tell them about it."

"The same goes for my supervisors," said Hobbes. "Our company is financially liable for this painting upwards of forty million dollars. They'll want to know as much as they can, as soon as they can."

"Actually," said Rivers. "I'm pretty sure they'll want the

painting recovered. That's true of your supervisors and of the trustees. Still, I understand the difficulty of your situations, which is why the director of the FBI is personally calling the chairman of the museum's board and the president of the insurance company. He's informing them about the theft and asking them, in his very convincing way, to keep it quiet so that we are in a better situation to capture the bad guys."

He waited to make sure there were no more complaints, but the mention of the director's involvement seemed to put an end to the protests.

"All right, then," he said. "This food's delicious, so let's keep eating and figure this out."

"Why do you want to keep it a secret?" asked Mom. "Wouldn't people knowing about it help put pressure on the thief?"

"Yes, but pressure's not what we want," he explained. "I want the opposite of pressure. Right now he thinks he's gotten away with the crime of the century. That's good. We didn't catch him at the recycling center because word had already gotten out that the other paintings were recovered. As long as he thinks we don't know about the Monet, he's far more likely to make a mistake. "

"What's the latest on the artist who painted it?" asked my father.

"According to our counterparts at Interpol, Pavel Novak has not been seen since he flew from Washington to Prague the night of the burglary. We suspect he's somewhere in the Czech Republic, but realistically he could be almost anywhere in Eastern Europe. We're working with local police agencies and also trying to check with sources who have connections inside EEL."

"That's the crime syndicate you mentioned at FBI Headquarters," said Mom.

"That's right," he replied. "The Eastern European League is involved in illegal activity throughout the region. Even if it wasn't involved in this particular case, it's almost certain to have a history with Novak or any associates he may have."

"What about the burglar?" asked Hobbes. "The custodian who went missing?"

"We're still following multiple leads, but so far we're frustrated by our lack of results," he admitted. "We've looked at all the custodians who've worked in the National Gallery in the last year and each one has a solid alibi. The same cleaning company provides custodial services to the Department of Labor, the Bureau of Engraving and Printing, and the National Archives, so we're looking into all of those employees as well, but there are hundreds of names."

The mention of the National Archives caught my attention, and I must have reacted because Agent Rivers stopped talking and looked at me.

"Florian? Is there something you'd like to say?"

"Not really," I replied. "It's just that when you mentioned the National Archives, it made me think of something. Actually, someone."

"Who?" my father asked.

"Earl," I replied. "I don't know his last name."

"Earl Jackson?" asked Serena. "The man who was working in the security center the night of the burglary?"

I nodded.

"He's been with the museum for ten years," she said. "I guarantee he had nothing to do with this."

"I didn't think he did," I replied. "It's just that he came to mind and I guess I made a face."

"Why?" asked Agent Rivers. "What does he have to do with the National Archives?"

"He told me he used to work there," I said. "He left for two years and said he begged Ms. Miller for his job back."

"Is that true?" asked Rivers.

"Yes," said Miller. "But I mean it when I say there's no way he's involved."

"Well, someone from your department is," said Hobbes.

"What's that supposed to mean?" she replied angrily.

"It's obvious," he answered.

"Let's not get into finger-pointing and accusations," said Rivers.

"Someone from your department has to be involved," Hobbes reiterated, ignoring the agent. "Someone had to tell the thief that the security system was going to be reset at precisely one fifteen."

"And you think it was Earl?" she replied.

"I have no idea if it was him," replied Hobbes. "I've only met him a few times so I don't know him. But I do know that he was in charge of the security upgrade the night the paintings were stolen. And now it turns out he has a connection to the National Archives, which may be important."

It was about to erupt into a full-fledged argument when my mother came to the rescue. "Who wants dessert?" she said. "Agent Rivers brought an apple crumb pie that looks delicious."

At first no one responded, so I jumped in.

"Do we have any ice cream to go with it?"

"Of course we do," she said.

"Sounds good to me," said Agent Rivers.

The pie did the trick and the argument was averted, although Hobbes and Miller exchanged angry looks with each other the rest of the evening. The focus of the conversation turned to the different types of people behind most art thefts.

"There are three basic types," said Rivers. "Knuckleheads, masterminds, and extortionists."

"What are knuckleheads?" I asked.

"Basic criminals, usually not so bright, who see an opportunity to steal a piece of art and take it," explained my father. "They're usually short on planning and have no idea what to do with what they take."

"They're also responsible for most of the art stolen throughout the world," added Ms. Miller.

"But I don't think that's what we're dealing with here," said Rivers. "Breaking a window and grabbing a picture off the wall is one thing. But creating a high-level forgery and swapping it with the original takes meticulous planning."

"Which leads us to mastermind," said Hobbes. "A crime in which a very rich person targets a specific piece of art to add to his collection."

"That could be the case here," speculated my mother. "*Woman with a Parasol* is iconic."

"No doubt," said Rivers. "But the truth is, the mastermind art thefts tend to be more of what you see in movies and less of what happens in real life."

"So you suspect extortion?" said Serena.

"I'm leaning that way," he said. "But I want to stay open-minded."

"What's extortion?" I asked.

Agent Rivers turned to Oliver Hobbes. "You want to tell him?"

"That's when criminal syndicates like EEL acquire a painting and then try to ransom it back to the insurance company or museum," he said. "Officially, insurance companies do not pay ransoms. But unofficially, they do offer rewards for information leading to the return of stolen paintings, which some people claim is really the same thing."

"Why would an insurance company pay that?" I asked.

"*Woman with a Parasol* is valued at roughly forty million dollars," he said. "That's what my company will have to pay the National Gallery if it's not recovered so that they can purchase something of equal value to replace it. But whoever has it can't sell it for that much on the black market because of its history. It's toxic. So if they offer to 'help find it' for two million, then they make a lot of money and we save thirty-eight million dollars."

"But that's not going to happen in this situation because we're going to catch the bad guys and get it back ourselves," Rivers claimed.

"I like your thinking," said Hobbes. "So will my bosses."

"How do we do it?" asked Ms. Miller.

"Each of us has to work a specific lead," he said. "I know you don't want to think that anyone at the museum might be involved, but it has to be considered. The thief did know that the security system was going to be shut down. Isolate who had that information and see how word might have gotten out. Also, keep an eye on your staff and watch for suspicious behavior. Remember, the thief thinks he's gotten away with it, so see if anyone is making big life changes with an eye on sudden money coming in."

She nodded. "Fine. I can do that."

I caught his eye as a signal to remind him of a conversation we had during the car ride home. "Oh, and can I get a record of who on the staff has traveled to Europe in the last three years?"

She gave him a confused look. "Why?"

"If there is someone from the museum involved, we have to figure out how he might have met Pavel Novak in the first place," he said. "He's never been to the US, so the odds are that meeting took place in Europe."

"Europe is an entire continent," she pointed out. "How can you possibly figure out if two people met each other?"

"I can't," he said. "But we have this genius at the Bureau. If anyone can figure it out, he can. His name is Johan Blankvort."

As he said it, he shot me a look.

"What do you want me to do?" asked Hobbes.

"You've dealt with extortionists before and know about the black market," Rivers said. "Put feelers out to see if there's been any chatter that might seem even the slightest bit connected to what we're dealing with."

"I've also got a database of every major art auction in the past twenty years," Hobbes said. "I'll dig around and see if anyone has expressed particular interest in Monet or the major Impressionist works."

"That's a great idea," Rivers said. "I'd love to get a copy if I could. I might show it to Johan."

"Of course."

Now Rivers turned to my parents.

"I know you don't have an official role in this investigation, but your brainpower and breadth of knowledge are greatly appreciated. If you think of anything, please let me know."

"Our pleasure," said Mom.

"Absolutely," said Dad.

"And remember," he said to everyone, "the key to this is that we keep it a secret. If word gets out, everything changes."

19.

Capitol Crush

THE NEXT MORNING I RODE MY BIKE TO DEAL Middle to watch the championship game of the U13 Washington Area Girls Soccer League. The match was played on the big field behind the school and when I got there I was amazed by how many people had turned out.

Margaret had already told me all about the team they were facing. The Capitol Crush had won back-to-back city championships and was looking to become the first team ever to win three in a row. They wore red-and-white-striped jerseys and their supporters hung a huge banner on the fence that read CRUSH IT!

I headed for the opposite sideline and found Margaret's

parents in a cluster of Dynamo fans. "Did I miss anything?" I asked.

"No," said Mrs. Campbell. "Your timing's perfect. They're just about to do the Tornado."

The Tornado.

Margaret had told me all about that too, but I didn't fully appreciate how cool it was until I saw it in person. It started with the team forming a tight circle in front of their goal. Their arms were wrapped around each other's shoulders and they swayed side to side and started chanting, "D-C-D, D-C-D," for DC Dynamo. They got louder and louder and swayed more and more until the circle looked like it was about to spiral out of control. Finally one of the girls let out a piercing yell and they scattered from the huddle and ran to their positions.

Everyone on our sideline went nuts.

"That was impressive. I'm glad I didn't miss that," I said when the noise died down. "Although I meant to get here earlier so I could give her a pep talk."

Her dad laughed. "It's probably best that you didn't."

"Why's that?" I asked.

"Margaret's not exactly . . . chatty . . . before a big game," he explained.

When I saw her face I instantly realized what he meant.

The girl I normally hung out with, the goofy, brainy girl who was always smiling, bore little resemblance to the one who lined up to play center midfielder. This one was oblivious to the world beyond the sidelines. She focused an intense stare straight ahead at her opponent while she loosened up her shoulders and gently rocked up and down on the balls of her feet. It was unnerving.

"Where have I seen that look before?" I asked.

"The zoo," replied her mother. "It's the same expression the tiger has right before feeding time."

We all laughed because it was true.

The game was exciting from start to finish, and both teams played great. The Crush scored early, but the Dynamo tied it up right before halftime. It was still 1–1 when Margaret moved up out of position, stole a pass between two defenders, and sprinted all alone toward the goal. Their keeper, who played brilliantly all game long, charged out to challenge her, but Margaret put on the brakes and chipped the ball over her head and sent it fluttering into the net.

"Did you see that?" Mrs. Campbell squealed, jumping up and down. "Did you see that?"

It was a memorable play, but nothing like the one the Capitol Crush pulled off in the final moments of the game.

They were awarded a free kick, and, desperate to tie the score and force overtime, all of their players moved forward and flooded the penalty area. Two of them even started arguing about who should take the kick. Then, in the middle of the argument, another player sneaked in and kicked the ball to the other side of the field.

It was a trick play designed to give one of their players an open shot and it worked perfectly. No one was near her as she got the ball and volleyed it to the top left corner of the goal. Everyone on the DC Dynamo had been caught off guard watching the argument.

Except for Margaret.

She'd slipped in behind the keeper and taken a spot on the goal line. As the ball rocketed toward the net, she jumped up and headed it just enough to send it over the crossbar. Both sidelines went bananas, while Mr. Campbell and I did so many high fives the palm of my hand turned red. Two minutes later the referee blew the whistle, ending the game, and Margaret's teammates swarmed around her.

Somewhere in the middle of the celebration, she looked toward the sideline and we locked eyes. It was the first time I saw her smile that day. It lasted only a second because two more players piled on top of her and they all tumbled to the ground. I knew the team was going to their coach's house for a party, so I said good-bye to Margaret's parents and headed for the bike rack.

The school is a massive, three-story brick building that seems even larger because it sits on the top of a hill. I walked around to the front and was unlocking my bike when I heard someone coming toward me. I looked up and saw that it was Margaret. Despite being exhausted from a grueling game in the summer heat, she had run all the way up the hill after me.

"Where are you going?" she asked in between deep breaths.

"Home," I said.

"Without saying anything to me?"

"I didn't want to interrupt the celebration," I explained. "I figured we'd talk later."

"You're my best friend, Florian. By definition that means you can't interrupt me. You're always a part of whatever I'm a part of."

It was, without a doubt, the nicest thing anyone had ever said to me.

"I'll remember that in the future," I said. "By the way. You were . . . Amazing . . . Incredible . . . Unbelievable. It took my breath away."

She grinned. "It was a good game, wasn't it?"

I laughed. "You could say that."

"Thanks for saving that last goal," she said. "I don't know if we could've held them off in extra time."

"What are you talking about?" I asked.

"Without you I never would have headed that ball over the crossbar."

"Yeah right."

"I mean it," she replied. "The two players who got into the argument, I'd noticed them whispering to each other right before that. I thought that was strange. Then I realized their best goal scorer was in the absolute wrong place, totally away from the play. So I ignored the big thing, which was the argument, and added up the little things."

"You mean you used . . ."

"TOAST," she said, finishing my sentence. "TOAST absolutely won that game."

Now I was the one who was grinning.

"I'm going to keep the trophy and all," she continued. "But I couldn't have done it without you."

I looked up at the entrance to the school. It was imposing with tall white columns and three pairs of dark blue doors.

"Two more days until we start," I said.

"You're not worried about Deal, are you?"

"I always worry about new schools," I answered.

"Don't. You're going to do great," she assured me.

"Why? Because the school's loaded with geeky kids who have mad mystery-solving skills?"

"No," she answered. "Because I'll be there."

"That should take care of it," I replied. "Now go back and get your trophy and have fun at the party."

"Okay. I'll see you later." She jogged back down the hill to where her teammates were waiting. When she reached them, they swarmed her all over again.

Despite her assurance, I was still a little nervous about starting at a new school. Again. Each time presented new challenges.

I was in no rush to get home, so I rode around the neighborhood for a while to get a better feel for it. First I went to a castle-looking building right by the campus called Fort Reno. It was used to defend Washington during the Civil War, and now it's a park. According to one of the information plaques, it's the highest point in the city. After that I had a couple slices of pepperoni and sausage at a pizzeria with free Ping-Pong and foosball.

I was just about to play a kid in foosball when I noticed a man watching me as he talked on a cell phone. He was thin and muscular with short red hair and aviator sunglasses. He was also the only person in the building who wasn't working, eating, or playing.

"You going to play?" the boy asked me.

"No," I said. "I just realized what time it is and have to get home."

Since the red-haired man was between the front door and me, I decided to slip out the back. Unfortunately, it opened onto an alley where there was another man waiting for me. He was tall and lean and wore the same sunglasses as the guy inside.

"Stop right there," he said.

I instantly thought back to Kayla's self-defense training and tried to get into position.

"Are you Johan Blankvort?" he asked.

At first I didn't recognize the fake identity I'd been given, so I barked, "No."

Then I thought about it for a second and said, "I mean, yes. I mean, who wants to know?"

"I'm Agent Chaffee of the Federal Bureau of Investigation," he said in that direct FBI way.

"And I'm Agent Kendall," said a voice from behind.

I turned and saw that the redhead had followed me out.

"Agent Rivers asked us to come and get you and bring you straight home."

Just then I heard a text signal on my phone.

"'That's him telling you to trust us," said Kendall. "I was just speaking to him on the phone."

I pulled my phone out of my pocket and indeed there was a text from Rivers: *It's okay. Go with them.*

"Okay," I said. "So what's going on?"

"He didn't tell us that," replied Chaffee. "He just said to get you."

They led me to a black SUV, and when I got in I saw that they'd already loaded my bike into the back.

"Hey, that was locked," I protested.

"You might want to get a new one," Chaffee said, tossing the lock to me. "This one was pretty easy to pick."

I started to ask how they found me when I remembered the tracking chip inside the SmarTrip card for the Metro. It took only a few minutes to make it to the house, and when we pulled up I saw the maroon hybrid parked in front. I was excited because I thought there might have been a big break in the case, so I hurried up the front steps and went inside.

"Florian?" my mother called out. "We're in the kitchen."

I found my parents sitting around the table with Agent Rivers and another agent I didn't recognize. They all looked worried.

"What's the matter?" I asked.

"Were you at a soccer game today?" Rivers asked. "On the field behind your school?"

"Yes," I said. "It was great. Margaret's team won the championship and—"

"Did you see this man when you were there?" he said, cutting me off as he placed a photograph on the table.

I picked it up and studied it. It looked like a surveillance picture taken from a distance with a long lens. The man looked both stylish and menacing at the same time. He had on a nice suit, but his face was tight and muscular.

"Not that I remember," I said. "But there were a lot of people."

"Well, he was there," he said. "And we think he may have been there because of you."

"Who is he?" I asked.

Rivers sighed before answering. "He's an EEL crime boss named Nicolae Nevrescu. But his enemies call him 'Nic the Knife.'"

"That sounds bad," I said with a gulp. "What do his friends call him?"

"He doesn't have any friends."

20.

The Underground

MY PARENTS AND I SPENT THE NEXT HALF HOUR learning all about Nicolae Nevrescu from Rivers and his fellow agent Martin Kellogg.

"Marty's really our expert on him," Rivers explained. "So I want him to tell you the basics."

Kellogg was about ten years older, and unlike the always-sharp Rivers, he was somewhat wrinkled and unkempt. He'd spent years sitting in the backs of surveillance vans tracking criminals and was a little worse for the wear.

"Although he's the son of a prominent Romanian mobster, the plan seems to have been to keep Nic out of the family business," he said with his New York accent. "He was smart, had a bright future, and his parents wanted him to go to America and start a new chapter in the family's history. He came to Washington as a student at Georgetown, majored in international business, made good grades, and was headed to law school."

"So how did he end up a gangster?" asked Dad.

"The how we don't know," he answered. "We just know that he did. With money from his dad, he opened a construction company that was corrupt from the beginning. In little over a decade, his businesses have grown to include everything from sanitation and recycling centers to demolition and dry-cleaning companies. All of them launder money for his father and other EEL crime lords."

"How do you launder money?" I asked.

"You take money earned through illegal activities and pass it through a legitimate business so it becomes clean," he explained.

"If you know all this," asked my mother, "then why don't you arrest him?"

"We want to," he answered. "But what we know and what we can prove in court are two different things. We've had him under surveillance for two years, and we're building a case against him."

"Which brings us to today," said Rivers. "The surveillance

team followed him to the soccer game at Deal."

"That's all?" I asked. "That's why you grabbed me off the street and terrified my parents? Because both of us were at a soccer game? There were a lot of people there. What makes you think he was there because of me? He could have been there to watch his kid. Or watch his friend's kid. It was a big game, the city championship."

"He doesn't have any kids, and he doesn't have any friends," said Kellogg. "All of his family is in Romania, and in two years he's never once shown the slightest interest in soccer or youth sports. But he did show an interest in you."

"What do you mean?" asked Dad.

"After the game, he walked around the school and watched Florian get on his bike and leave." Kellogg handed a photograph to my mom and dad, and I leaned over from my seat to look at it. In the picture, I was watching Margaret as she ran back down the hill to her team, and he was about twenty-five yards behind me. It was weird seeing a picture of myself that I hadn't known was being taken.

"I still think you're taking a big leap," I replied. "The parking lot in front of the school was full of cars. He could have been looking at anything. He may not have even noticed me and just happened to be facing that direction."

"You're absolutely right," said Rivers. "This may well be

an overreaction. In fact, it probably is. But we'd rather over-react and err on the side of safety than make a mistake and put you in jeopardy."

"We agree," said Mom.

"Definitely," added Dad.

I turned to Kellogg and asked, "How did you even know I was there? I thought I was a covert asset."

"The chip on your SmarTrip card," answered Rivers. "There's always the worry that a surveillance op might blow someone's cover. So there's a monitor in the van that picks up the signal from anyone with a chip like yours."

"I still didn't know who you were," added Kellogg. "But when the monitor displayed a number, I called it in to the covert asset desk to let them know our two situations had overlapped. They called Rivers."

"And when I heard it involved Nevrescu and EEL, it set off the alarm in the little monitor in my head," he said. "Since we suspect that EEL is involved in the theft, we decided to act."

The pieces may have snapped together for them, but they didn't for me. It seemed like a total stretch. Although I will admit that may have been because I didn't want to think that the Romania Mafia might be coming after me. But it still seemed unlikely.

"Does it make sense that he'd be interested in art?" I asked Kellogg.

"He's not your average criminal," he replied. "He graduated from Georgetown and is intellectual. He supports various cultural activities in the Romanian-American community. He even created a scholarship fund, totally legitimate, that helps inner-city DC kids go to college. So a Monet might appeal to him a great deal."

"Besides, his interest wouldn't necessarily be in the artistic value of the painting," added Rivers. "In the world of organized crime, stolen art is often used in place of money to pay off one group or another."

"So what do we do about it?" asked Mom as she reached over and put a protective hand on my knee.

"First of all, Florian's off the case," he said.

"What?" I protested.

"Stay away from any place and anyone associated with the crime or the investigation," he continued. "If he was there to see you, he most likely just heard a rumor that you were involved and was curious to find out how. We don't want to give him any reason to believe that rumor's true. If you stay away from the museum and the investigation, he'll lose interest quickly."

"If Florian's a covert asset, then how could Nevrescu

even hear a rumor about him?" asked Mom.

"That night at the museum, there were a lot of people there when Florian figured out where the paintings were hidden," he said. Then he turned to me and asked, "Do you want to tell them which ones might have told Nevrescu?"

"How would I know?" I replied.

He gave me a look and leaned in. "Do you want to tell them, Florian? Because I think you know."

"You haven't told anyone, have you?" Dad asked me.

"No. Of course not," I replied. "He's talking about the guys on the garbage truck."

"I figured you caught that," Rivers said with a smile.

"Okay, for those of us who aren't detectives?" asked my mom.

"The garbage truck drivers were there on the scene being questioned as the agents dug through the Dumpsters looking for the paintings," I reminded her. "They were there when the agents gave me the standing ovation. And Agent Kellogg said that Nevrescu owns sanitation and recycling centers. So there's a possible connection."

"Impressive," said Agent Kellogg.

"I told you," replied Rivers.

"What about the stuff from the dinner party?" I asked. "You said you wanted me to use TOAST to analyze the travel records from the museum to see who had traveled to Europe on business and to look over the information Oliver Hobbes had about auctions involving Monet and the Impressionists. Neither of those involves Nevrescu. Can I still do that?"

Rivers looked at my parents as if to gauge their response.

"I can look at them here at the house," I added. "The sooner this case is solved, the better all of this will be."

"I guess that would be all right with me," said Rivers. "If it's okay with your parents."

Dad nodded. "That would be okay. He's safe here."

One of the advantages of having a father who designs security systems is that our house is super well protected. We had video surveillance, door and window sensors, motion detectors, exterior lighting, alarms, and anything else you could think of. We even had special high-security cables for Internet access, which was necessary because my dad runs his business from home.

They stayed for a little while more and reminded me about fifteen times to make sure I always carried my panic button with me. The next morning I went down into the unfinished room in our basement and started turning it into the world headquarters of Florian Bates Investigations. If I was going to have to work out of the house, then I wanted to at least have a good place to do it.

I was staring at one of the walls when I heard a voice behind me.

"What are you doing?"

I turned to see that it was Margaret. "Interior decorating."

She laughed. "Well, now I know."

"What?" I asked.

"Now I know the thing you're really bad at is interior decorating."

I nodded. "I am, aren't I?"

"Terrible," she said.

I had just been trying to squeeze as much into each corner as I could, but then Margaret took over and started "using the negative space," as she said. Over the next four hours it went from a room with boxes to a cool environment where we could brainstorm and work cases together. She made one wall into a giant case board and turned the gaps under the stairs into funky staggered shelving.

While we worked I told her all about Nic the Knife, stressing my belief that he wasn't involved and accusing my parents and Agent Rivers of overreacting.

"They're not overreacting," she retorted. "They're being careful and that's smart."

She got onto the computer, which sat on a desk we made out of an old door and some wooden boxes, and started looking up everything she could about Nevrescu. I'd done the same thing the night before so I'd already seen most of what she came across.

"Here's an article about his scholarship fund," she said. "He looks intense."

"Is that the picture of him by the bridge with his arms crossed?" I asked as I tried to figure out the best place to put a floor lamp.

"That's the one," she said.

"He definitely has a don't-mess-with-me vibe," I said.

"And that's in an article about him helping kids go to college," she joked. "Imagine how he looks when he's trying to be intimidating."

"How's this?" I moved out of the way so she could see where I'd put the lamp.

"Uh-uh," she replied, shaking her head. "Over there."

She pointed at the other corner.

I moved the lamp and she kept looking online.

"*Mi-ar placea sa vizitez Romania,*" she said. Well, that's what she tried to say. What she actually said was a much-butchered version of that.

"What's that?" I asked.

"It's Romanian for 'I'd like to visit Romania one day,'" she answered. "Here's a website of Romanian phrases. It might help if you learned some in case you two come face-to-face someday. I wonder how you say 'No, I didn't have anything to do with uncovering your plot to steal tens of millions of dollars of paintings. Please don't hurt me.'" She pretended to look at the list and said, "No, I guess that's not a common enough phrase."

"Let me look at that," I said.

I looked over her shoulder at the phrases. It's funny because Romanian has a lot in common with Italian, so I could actually make sense of most of the phrases.

"Check this one out," she said, pointing to one at the bottom. "My hovercraft is full of monkeys." She laughed when she read that. "You definitely have to learn that one. You never know when that'll come in handy."

We both got up to leave, and when we reached the door, we turned around to look at the room. It was much cooler than I would have imagined.

"What do you think?" she asked.

"I love it," I replied. "How about you?"

"Almost," she said. "But it's missing something."

She knelt down and started looking through a box filled with odds and ends from our many moves.

"Should we give it a name?" I asked.

"What? The room?"

"Yeah, should we give it a name? In London, the police work out of Scotland Yard."

"And in Gotham City, Bruce Wayne's got the Batcave," she offered.

"Exactly," I answered, going with it. "We need a name like that."

I tried to brainstorm, and she kept digging through the box.

"Wait a minute, I think I've got it," she said.

She pulled out a metal sign that had the symbol of the London subway system. It was classic and simple. A red circle with a blue bar across the middle. The word "Underground" was written in the bar.

"I like it," I said.

She hung it from an old nail in the wall and stepped back to look at everything.

"It's perfect," she said. "Welcome to the Underground."

21.

Back to School

IT WAS THE FIRST DAY OF SCHOOL AND MOM wanted to drive. This had nothing to do with her being worried about Nicolae Nevrescu, and everything to do with the fact that she's a mom and thinks I'm still in kindergarten.

"It's less than a mile away," I said. "I can just walk with Margaret."

"Why don't I drive Margaret, too?" she offered.

"Because then her mother will feel left out and she'll want to drive," I answered. "We'd end up with two cars when we don't need any."

"Okay, but if I don't drive, then I get to take a first-day-of-school picture in front of the house," she said, suddenly turning it into a negotiation. "And one with a real smile, not the I'm-twelve-and-hate-having-my-picture-taken pretend smile."

I carefully considered her offer. "Are you going to post the picture online?"

"I'm going to post some picture online," she said. "It will either be this one or that adorable one of you as a baby dancing in a diaper. I'll let you pick."

She's a tough negotiator, my mother.

"All right, then," I said, cutting my losses. "Let's take some pictures."

I posed for a few solo shots and a couple more with Margaret. Once Mom was satisfied, Margaret and I started walking. We'd made it to the end of the driveway when Mom called out random encouragement: "Seventh grade will be seventh heaven! Be your true self! I love you!"

I turned to face her. "That's why you can't drive me on the first day, Mom. Because you say stuff like that. Out loud. Where people can hear."

"I know. It's just that I care so much."

"I know you do, Mom."

"Don't worry, Mrs. B.," Margaret said. "I'll keep an eye on him."

We waved good-bye and started down the sidewalk—

although I can't be certain Mom didn't secretly follow us in her car.

"Sorry about that," I said to Margaret once we were far enough away.

"Are you kidding?" she replied. "At seven fifteen I was in the middle of a video chat with my grandmother so she could see my outfit."

It's always hard to start at a new school, but at least it wasn't in the middle of the year. We moved to London in February and that was a total nightmare. I got the worst seat in every classroom and never really found a group of friends.

This time I had high hopes. I also had Margaret helping guide the way and answering any questions. Like when we walked through the front door and I saw the security setup.

"Metal detectors and X-ray machines?" I asked. "Is this an everyday thing?"

She shrugged like it was no big deal. "You get used to it. They use them throughout the District."

"The school's safe, isn't it?"

"Totally," she said. "Besides, this will help keep out any strangers, you know, like the Romanian Mafia."

I laughed. "Well, when you put it that way, I guess it's a good thing."

Because Deal was so large, each grade was split into

teams of five teachers and about a hundred students. The teams were named after major international cities and we were assigned to Team Cairo.

Margaret and I had three classes together: English, ancient history, and algebra. But more important, we were both in the same lunch. Breakfast may be the most important meal of the day nutritionally speaking, but lunch is the one that matters the most when it comes to socializing. It really helps to have a friend.

The biggest struggle I had that first week had nothing to do with schoolwork or making friends, and everything to do with coming back to reality. I'd just spent a summer during which I went to the FBI training academy, helped discover a spy ring trying to infiltrate the CIA, and been part of the investigation into nearly $100 million in stolen paintings. And now I was a seventh grader.

Just a seventh grader.

I was a normal kid in a class full of normal kids, and I couldn't even tell anyone about all the cool adventures. My English teacher asked us to write about what happened over the summer and I couldn't think of anything interesting that hadn't been classified by the government.

The most exciting moment came on Tuesday afternoon when Margaret and I were walking home from school. She kept a constant lookout for anyone suspicious and was certain the man in the slow-moving Volkswagen was an EEL operative. When he stopped and got out of his car, she was prepared to, as she put it, "unleash the fury of my kung fu." Luckily she managed to stop herself when we realized he was delivering a pizza to the house we were standing in front of.

"Do you normally unleash that power with or without pepperoni?" I asked as we both struggled to keep a straight face.

By Friday even she was no longer concerned about the Romanian Mafia. On Saturday afternoon I was in full sprawl on the couch watching television when Mom asked me if I had any homework.

"Five pages of algebra and five hundred words about my summer," I said.

"How close are you to being done?" she asked.

I smiled. "I've got the whole weekend to do it. I haven't even started."

She gave me that Mom look and said, "Too bad."

"Why?" I asked.

"Because our deal was that you couldn't save the country until after you'd finished your homework."

I shot upright on the couch. "What? Is there work for me to do? Detective work?"

She held up two manila envelopes. "Agent Rivers had these dropped off today."

"Let me see them," I said.

She held them out for me, but then snapped them back as I reached for them. "Let me see your homework."

I got the point and instantly turned off the television and rushed upstairs to get my backpack. "I'll have it done right away," I promised.

"No, you'll have it done *right*," she corrected. "Do not rush your homework. I'm going to check everything before I consider it done."

The algebra went pretty quickly, but the five hundred words were a different story. I didn't know what to write. Like I said, all the cool stuff was classified, so I decided to write about our move to America and the change of culture.

"Pffftt," Mom said after she read it. "There's nothing there."

"That's because nothing happened," I said. "Except for the FBI stuff, but I can't write about that."

"Nothing happened, huh?" she said. "Well, this is your first chance to let anyone at the school get to know you."

"Not really," I replied. "Margaret knows me."

"She does?" said my mother. "When did she get to know you?"

"This summer . . ." My words trailed off when I realized what she was trying to do.

"I guess something did happen," she replied.

I went back upstairs and wrote about my friendship with Margaret. I didn't make it all gushy. I just started writing about things we did, and by the time I stopped to take a look, I'd already finished 627 words.

"*Magnifico*," Mom said when she read it. "If you'd like I can give you one of the pictures I took of the two of you and you can turn it in with the essay."

"Thanks, but no thanks, Mom."

Margaret came over the next morning and we went down into the basement to start working. Agent Rivers had sent two envelopes. One had a record of every museum employee who had traveled to Europe on official business over the past three years. The other had records of all the auctions for major works of Impressionism going back five years.

"Which do you want to do first?" I asked.

"Let's start with the travel," she said.

Our goal with the travel was to figure out how someone at the museum might have met Pavel Novak.

"Let's look at who went to conventions and expositions," I said. "That's the most likely place for them to have bumped into each other."

"Sounds good," said Margaret.

"I got this list of them from my mom," I said. "She's a member of some art group and gets invited to all of them."

The fact that the room was unfinished is what made the Underground such a great place to work. We didn't have to worry about ruining anything like the paint on the wall, because there wasn't any paint on the wall. So Margaret wrote the name and date of each convention on separate index cards and taped them to the walls.

"Now let's see which of these dates and places line up with trips by museum staff," she said.

At first none of the dates lined up, which didn't make any sense. After all, someone had to at least go to some meeting.

"I got it," I said when I realized what we'd done wrong. "The dates on the travel documents are in the American style and the dates on the events are European."

"We use different dates?" she asked.

"Americans write the month first and then the day, while Europeans write the day first and then the month. So June thirteenth is 6/13 in America, and it's 13/6 in Europe."

When we fixed this, all of the trips lined up perfectly.

"So in the last three years, there were seven conventions where museum staff went to Europe," Margaret said, looking at our wall.

"Any of them in the Czech Republic?" I asked hopefully.

"No," she said. "Two of them were in London, and the others were in Munich, Copenhagen, Florence, Budapest, and Warsaw."

"Okay, so that's where the staff went," I said, thinking out loud. "Which ones would Pavel Novak go to? He was a star student at the Academy of Fine Arts in Prague. He wants to find a job. He wants to get hired to paint."

"Then that knocks out Copenhagen," said Margaret. "Because it's a forum for fund-raising, and Munich, because it's just for security people."

"That's good," I said as I took those lists down. "Now we're down to five."

"And we can eliminate Florence, too," said Margaret.

"How?"

"Because the only person to go to that one was a curator named Michael Jennings," she said. "And according to the museum's website, he left to work at the Metropolitan Museum of Art in New York over a year ago."

We'd cut the list to four, but it still felt a little needle-in-a-haystack-ish. We just sat there stumped and stared at the wall.

"By the way," I said, "I wanted to warn you that my mother posted those first-day-of-school pictures of us online and now all my relatives want to meet you when they visit. So be prepared to get swarmed at the holidays."

"I can handle it," she said. "That's the danger of social media."

That gave me an idea. I hopped up and went over to the computer.

"What are you doing?"

"Checking social media," I answered.

"I thought we were working," she protested.

"This is work," I told her. "Maybe mothers aren't the only ones who share too much. What if schools do too?"

I typed in "Academy of Fine Arts in Prague."

"Check it out," I said when the results filled the screen.

We spent the next twenty minutes scrolling through all of the pictures, posts, tweets, and mentions the academy had put up. We found what we were looking for in a picture posted fifteen months earlier.

"Alumni get-together at ArtFest in Budapest," said the caption.

"Top row, third from the left," I said. "I think that's our boy."

Margaret leaned in close to get a good look, and when she turned to face me, she had a big smile. "Got him!"

I got up and went to the wall where we'd taped the roster for the ArtFest in Budapest.

"Who do we have?" she asked.

I started reading off the names. "Michael Jennings, Kendra May, Ryan Thigpen . . ."

The bottom two took my breath away.

"Who is it?"

I held up the paper and said, "Serena Miller and Earl Jackson."

22.

Extra-Credit Algebra

I COULDN'T BELIEVE THAT SERENA MILLER AND Earl Jackson could possibly be involved in the theft of *Woman with a Parasol*.

Or maybe I just didn't want to believe it.

Miller was a family friend and Jackson was so nice and unassuming he insisted I call him by his first name. But I also couldn't ignore the fact that both were at ArtFest in Budapest at the same time as Pavel Novak.

"It could just be a coincidence," offered Margaret. "Remember when you were first teaching me about TOAST? You warned me that just because something is unexpected, doesn't mean it's suspicious."

"Yes, but it's the closest we've come to connecting Novak with anyone at the museum," I said. "Even worse, they were both directly involved with updating the security software. You couldn't pick anyone in a better position to orchestrate the whole burglary."

I sat down in my chair and slumped.

"I haven't met either one of them, so I don't know what they're like," she said. "But there were three other people from the museum at that convention. What about them?"

These were the names and titles listed on the itinerary:

**Michael Jennings, PhD, Curator
Kendra May, Conservator
Ryan Thigpen, Project Manager
Serena Miller, Director of Security
Earl Jackson, Security Manager**

"We know it's not Jennings because he moved to New York over a year ago to work at the Metropolitan Museum of Art," I said.

"What about the other two?" Margaret asked. "If Kendra May is a conservator, then she probably works with your mom."

"You're right," I said. "Let's find out."

We headed upstairs and found Mom in the front yard

painting a picture of the house. It's a tradition she's done of every home we've lived in.

"Wow," Margaret said, admiring it. "That's beautiful, Mrs. B."

Mom smiled. "Thanks. It may not be nice enough for the National Gallery, but we should be able to find a spot for it somewhere in the house."

"Don't let her modesty fool you," I said. "She's sold paintings in some really nice galleries."

"And don't let sales fool you," she responded. "Van Gogh only sold two paintings in his entire life. We could talk for hours about the difference between what's true art and what sells. But I don't think that's why you came up here. You look like you have a question."

"Two actually," I said. "Do you know a project manager named Ryan Thigpen?"

She thought about it for a moment. "The name's familiar. But I don't know him. I think he oversees modern-art installations in the East Building."

"What about Kendra May?"

"Of course," said Mom. "Kendra's extremely talented. She specializes in the Impressionists and the Postimpressionists, like I do. She did an amazing job repairing a Degas that had been damaged in storage."

"So if her specialty is the Impressionists, then she'd be a fan of Monet, right?" reasoned Margaret.

"Who isn't a fan of Monet?" answered Mom. "But sure. In fact, I think she did some academic research about him for her PhD."

So far, so good.

"What's she like as a person?" I asked. "Is she nice?"

Mom laughed a little as she considered this. "She's not mean. But she's also not too friendly. She likes to do her own thing. And she really gets upset if anyone moves her lunch in the break room refrigerator."

Margaret and I shared a look. I already liked her much more as a candidate than Serena and Earl.

"Why do you ask?" Mom wanted to know.

"It's part of what I'm looking into for Agent Rivers," I said. "It turns out she was at a convention in Hungary at the same time as the man who painted the forgery of *Woman with a Parasol*."

"And you think she might be involved?" asked Mom.

I shrugged. "Maybe."

"Well then, I have bad news," she said. "Kendra had a baby a few days before the burglary. A boy named Vincent."

Suddenly, Kendra May seemed much less likely to be the one we were looking for. I can't imagine anyone planning a major museum heist to coincide with giving birth. It would just make everything too unpredictable.

Margaret and I grabbed some apples from the kitchen and headed back to the basement.

"Here's what I'm thinking," Margaret said as we got back to work. "You're not going to meet someone and instantly hatch a plan to rob the National Gallery. You'd want to meet at least another time or two."

"That's true," I said. "So let's go back to all the records and see who went back to Europe."

This time we didn't consider only convention and trade show trips. We looked at all travel involving any of our potential candidates.

"Here's one for Ryan Thigpen," said Margaret. "Stockholm, Sweden, in January of this year."

"That sounds unbearably cold," I replied. "Anything for Kendra May?"

"No," she said. "I'm thinking that and the baby give her a pretty good alibi."

I was scanning through the papers when I came across a trip to Berlin by Earl Jackson. "Four days meeting with consultants," I said, reading off the description on the trip.

"Oh no," said Margaret.

"What is it?"

"Two trips by Serena Miller," she said, looking up at me. "One last September and one just a few weeks before we saw Novak in the museum."

"Where to?" I asked.

"The first one to Paris and the second Prague."

TOAST is about the accumulation of many little details, and for the moment at least, those details weren't looking too good for Serena. I was bummed, so Margaret reminded me that we had an entirely different lead to follow.

"You never know how it all might shake out," she said. "Let's see if the auctions show us anything interesting."

Because his insurance company worked with all the prestigious auction houses, Oliver Hobbes had been able to access complete bidding records for major auctions involving the big names of Impressionism. Normally, the public only finds out who winds up with the painting. But this gave us a much bigger picture of who was interested in the paintings the burglar targeted. We hoped we could find a mastermind hidden among the bidders.

"Each auction is printed on a separate piece of paper," I said to Margaret. "So let's line them up in chronological order."

Just like we'd done with the names of the conventions, we taped the results of each auction on the wall. This way we could walk along the evidence and look at the big picture instead of only bit by bit on a computer screen.

"I want to put pictures of the paintings up too," said Margaret. "That'll help me keep track of them in my brain."

"Good idea," I said.

Margaret got the images off the web and printed thumbnail copies of each. "There," she said as she taped the last one up. "It's like Gallery Eighty-Five has come to the Underground."

At first it was hard to look past anything but the massive sums of money paid out at the auctions. One of Monet's water lily paintings sold for $47 million to a private collector, while a museum paid $32 million for a portrait by Renoir.

"We're talking mad, crazy money," said Margaret. "And we think one of these people may be the mastermind?"

"Not one of the winners," I said. "Someone who can pay forty-seven million dollars for a painting doesn't need to steal one. We're looking for one of the losers. Someone who keeps trying to get one but gets outbid."

"So, if you can't beat 'em, cheat 'em?" she said.

"You got it."

Basically there were four different types of bidders: institutions such as museums looking to add the paintings to their collections, monetary funds and banks buying them as financial investments, private collectors, and what were called "anonymous entities."

"Why be an anonymous entity?" asked Margaret.

"A lot of reasons, I guess. Maybe you don't want anyone to know how much money you have. Maybe you don't want the art world to know which artists you're interested in. Or maybe . . ."

". . . you're a criminal who wants to keep his identity hidden," she said.

"Yeah," I agreed. "Maybe that."

We decided to focus on the anonymous bids.

"In order to stay anonymous, you have to hire a representative to do the actual bidding and communicating with the auction house," I explained to Margaret. "So what you do is give your representative a limit—say five million dollars—and the representative stays in the bidding until the price goes over the limit."

"That's why so many of these end on nice round numbers," she said pointing at one of the bid sheets. "This bidder stopped at ten million dollars. And this one stopped at fifteen million. Those must have been the limits their client gave them."

"Exactly," I said.

"So why did this one stop at 12,457,493 dollars?" she asked, pointing at a bid for a Monet.

I looked at it for a moment and said, "I have no idea."

She looked at an auction six months later. "Here's the same representative, American Art and Antique Acquisitions, trying to get another painting, also a Monet. The final bid is 12,629,127 dollars."

"Those are such random numbers," I said, completely baffled.

We looked through all the auctions and found nine instances when American Art and Antique Acquisitions tried to purchase a painting. Each time the painting was either a Monet or a Renoir. And each time the bidding stopped at a seemingly random number.

We wrote the bids on a separate sheet of paper and hung it on the wall, too. Then we just sat there and stared at it. And stared. And stared. As if the answer might jump out at us.

"Argghhh," Margaret said, rubbing her temples. "It's like I'm doing extra-credit algebra homework."

"Maybe that's it," I said. "Maybe it's algebra."

"What type of algebra?"

I got on the computer to search for something. "Here it is. Write this down: 'Amount to' equals 'amount from' times 'rate from' over 'rate to.'"

I looked up and she was giving me a total stink eye.

"I speak English, not equations," she said. "Why don't you just copy down what you see on the screen? And then explain what the heck you're talking about."

"Exchange rates. I dealt with them all the time when I lived in Europe. We'd have to figure out how many dollars are in a euro. Or if we went to London we'd have to convert euros into pounds. Maybe these actually are nice round numbers," I said, pointing at the list. "Just not in dollars."

I tried doing the math on paper until Margaret reminded me that the computer would be quicker. I started entering numbers into the equations, and then I compared those amounts with currency rates from the days of each auction. It was complicated, but when I was done it couldn't have been more basic. Each number equaled the exact same amount.

"Fifty million leu," I said.

"Fifty-million what?" she asked, confused.

"Leu. It's a type of money."

"Oh," she said. "Which country uses the leu?"

That's when I grinned. "Romania."

23.

An Actor Named
John Wilkes Booth

ONCE NICOLAE NEVRESCU ENTERED THE STORY,
preserving my covert status became more essential. I wasn't
allowed to call or text Agent Rivers, and I certainly couldn't
just show up at the Hoover Building and ask to see him. If I
wanted to make contact, he told me I needed to do so by way
of a website made especially for people like me.

"You mean secret agents?" I asked, charged with excitement.

"No, I mean middle schoolers," he answered, bringing
me back to earth.

The FBI Kids Page is a site for students who want to
learn about the Bureau. It has video clips, interactive games,
animations, and a link called "Ask an Agent."

I clicked the link and signed in as twelve-year-old Johan Blankvort of Bethesda, Maryland. My question: "How can you meet an agent in person?" Soon I received a standard response that told me about community outreach programs, such as the demonstrations put on by the FBI's K-9 Explosives Detection team, where agents were available to the public. Then, the next morning while Margaret and I were walking to school, I got a text from a phone number I didn't recognize. It read:

> Tell Johan to visit Our American Cousin after school today.

That was it. I waited for another text that might, you know, explain what that one meant, but none came.

"Who's that from?" Margaret asked.

"Agent Rivers."

"What's he have to say?"

Sigh. "I have absolutely no idea."

She read the text and asked, "Who's Johan?"

"I am. Johan Blankvort is my secret identity with the Bureau."

"Get out!" She stopped in her tracks and turned to face me. "You have an actual government-issued secret identity?"

"I've even got fake IDs," I said, fighting back an ear-to-ear grin.

"That may be the coolest thing I've ever heard," she replied. "But if you're Johan, then who's your American cousin?"

I spent most of the day trying to figure that out. I must have reread the text a hundred times. Including once during life science, which cost me three class-participation points. But it wasn't until lunch that I paid attention to the fact that the words "Our American Cousin" were all capitalized.

"You think that's important?" Margaret asked when I pointed it out to her. "People are kind of random when it comes to punctuation in texts."

"Agent Rivers isn't random about anything," I countered. "If it's capitalized, it must be the title of something."

I googled "Our American Cousin" and found that it was the name of the play Abraham Lincoln was watching the night he was assassinated.

Now I knew what I was supposed to do.

After school, I got on the Metro and took the Red Line to Gallery Place. (I'm guessing the instant I used my SmarTrip card a message alerted Agent Rivers I was on my way.) From the subway station it was just a short walk to Ford's Theatre.

On April 14, 1865, Abraham Lincoln went to Ford's to watch a performance of *Our American Cousin*. During the play's third act, he was shot by John Wilkes Booth. Now it was a historic site run by the National Park Service.

It also happened to be right around the corner from FBI Headquarters.

I got my ticket and blended in with all the tourists walking through the exhibits that detailed the events leading up to the president's death. I was looking at the actual derringer pistol Booth used to kill him when the man standing next to me asked a question.

"How long did it take you to figure out where we were meeting?"

I glanced up and saw that it was Agent Rivers.

"Most of the day," I said. "And I got in trouble for looking at my phone during class."

"Sorry about that," he said. "But I knew you'd solve it."

If anyone happened to notice us, we just looked like tourists on vacation. He'd swapped his normal suit and tie for a Nationals T-shirt and a pair of jeans. For the most part, we didn't even look at each other. We just kept our eyes on the exhibits and talked quietly.

"So, what did you find out?" he asked.

"A lot," I replied. "Last year Pavel Novak and five staff members from the National Gallery were at the same trade show in Budapest."

"Anyone we know on that trip?" he asked.

"Earl Jackson . . . and Serena Miller."

I could see his reflection in the exhibit glass and his reaction was as surprised as mine had been.

"Really? Earl and Serena?"

"It gets worse. Miller took two more trips to Europe, including one to Prague two weeks before Novak entered the country."

"That's . . . interesting."

"I keep thinking back to when Earl's name came up at the dinner party. She was so adamant that he couldn't be involved. I thought it was because she trusted him. But maybe she was just worried that if we pursued him, it would lead to her as well."

"What about the auctions?"

"More good news," I said. "It turns out an anonymous bidder has tried—and failed—to acquire a major Impressionist work at nine different auctions. He's put up a lot of money and is no doubt frustrated that he keeps losing."

"If the bidder's anonymous, how does it help us?" asked Rivers.

"Well, we know that the money is coming from Romania," I said. "And also that the bids were placed by a company here in Washington."

"So it could be Nevrescu laundering the money for his father?"

I nodded.

"I looked him up some more," I said. "He really likes to get involved in cultural events. Especially ones in the Romanian-American community."

"Right."

"So in two weeks there's an open house at the Romanian embassy. They're calling it a festival of food and family. He's one of the sponsors of the event. He'll be there."

"Maybe," said Rivers. "But we sure won't."

"Why not?" I asked. "It's a chance to interact with him in public. A chance to see who he's meeting with."

"We already have him under surveillance a lot of the time," he reminded me. "So we know most of the people he meets with. But more important, we're not allowed to go inside an embassy."

"You're the FBI. You can go anywhere you want."

"In America," he said. "But as soon as you set foot onto embassy grounds, by law you are in that country. If I tried to investigate someone while they were in that building, it would be seen as a violation of their sovereignty. Before you know it, the State Department's involved and there's an international incident."

"Oh," I said, slightly embarrassed. "I didn't realize the legal part of it."

"That's okay. You're the kid and I'm the FBI agent. I'm the one who's *supposed* to know that," he told me. "But you've done an amazing job, Florian. You've given us a lot to build on."

"I love doing it," I told him. "What can I work on next?"

He looked at me, sighed, and put his hand on my shoulder. Past experience told me I wasn't going to like what he said next.

"Nothing," he answered. "You can't do anything involving the *Woman with a Parasol* case. I don't even want you working on it at home."

I was devastated.

"But you just said I'd done an amazing job."

"You have," he said. "But we can't risk your safety. The more likely it is that Nevrescu is involved, the more likely it is that you're in danger."

"Why? Just because we were both at the same soccer game?"

"I'm sorry, Florian. But that's more than enough for me."

"But it was just a coincidence," I argued. "There were tons of people there. Besides, if he wanted to do anything to me, don't you think he would have just done it then, when he had the chance?"

Rather than answer, Rivers turned toward the enlarged picture on display in front of us. "This photograph was taken at Abraham Lincoln's second inauguration," he said, "six weeks before he was killed."

The photo was of a massive crowd on the steps of the Capitol Building. In the middle of them all, you could see Abraham Lincoln, standing behind a podium reading his speech.

"Lincoln's in the middle, but do you know who this is?"

He pointed to a man in the crowd of people looking down on the president from behind.

"No. Who is it?"

"He's an actor named John Wilkes Booth," he said. "But there were tons of people there. And besides, if he wanted to hurt the president, don't you think he would have done it when he had a chance?"

I stood there silently and considered what he was saying.

"You tell me," said Rivers. "You think him being there was a coincidence?"

24.

Let's Play TOAST

WHEN AGENT RIVERS SAID I WAS OFF THE CASE, he meant it. As soon as I started to leave Ford's Theatre, it was as if we'd never met. I turned back to say good-bye, but he'd already disappeared through some unseen exit.

As the days passed, I had no idea if the leads I'd given him helped or if the case had taken a dramatic turn or maybe even hit a dead end. I constantly checked news sites to see if there were any breaking stories about Romanian mobsters being arrested, and every day I'd wait anxiously for my mother to get home from work, just in case she might have heard a rumor or maybe seen federal agents sealing off Serena Miller's office.

My only connection to the investigation was in the Underground, where I still had my own case board on the wall. I tinkered with it all the time, straightening the cards, reorganizing them. Hoping I might stumble onto some perfect alignment that revealed the mastermind.

I was trying out a color-coding system for the cards when I heard someone hustling down the stairs to the basement. Seconds later, Margaret burst into the room in full-Margaret mode.

"I just had a genius idea!"

"What is it?" I asked expectantly. "Does it have to do with *Woman with a Parasol*? Finding your birth parents? Did you figure out how to find one of the long-lost firefighters?"

"No, no, and no. It has to do with you."

"Okay," I said, my enthusiasm slightly dampened. After all, I'm far less interesting than all those things. Still, I was happy that something was about to break the boredom. "What's your idea?"

"You're running for student council."

I waited to see if there was any more to this brainstorm, but I could tell by her expression and the awkward silence that she had put it all out there.

"What's . . . student council?" I asked warily.

"What do you mean, 'what's student council?'?"

"I think the question's pretty self-explanatory," I said.

"Have you been living under a rock or something?" she asked.

"No, but I have been living in Europe for the last eight years," I reminded her. "I don't think they have student council there. At least not at the schools where I went."

"That's too bad, because it's really cool. There are two representatives from each homeroom and they get to help plan the school dances and organize fund-raisers, and at the end of the year they take a trip to Kings Dominion. We're talking epic roller coasters."

"Dances, fund-raisers, roller coasters?" I said, listing three things I considered far more terrifying than the Romanian Mafia. Although, for the record, I had yet to confess any of these fears to Margaret.

"So what do you think?" she asked expectantly.

"I . . . don't know." I tried to fake a little enthusiasm but the best I could do was "Maybe?"

"Why *maybe*? It'll be a great way to make new friends and it's a lot of fun."

"Really? Because it doesn't sound like a lot of fun. It sounds like . . . a lot of work."

She plopped into a chair and all the oomph seemed to drain from her body. "I don't know how to break this to you,

Florian, but in the world of twelve-year-olds, that stuff is fun. I know you got to be a part of something huge. And I think there are going to be times when you get to do that again. I mean, you're a consulting detective with the FBI! That's amazing. But it's also a part-time job. You can't just sit around rearranging the cards on your case board, waiting for a mysterious text."

She looked up at the case board for a moment and smiled. "Although I see what you're doing with the color coding and I think it may be game changing."

"It works, doesn't it?" I said, glad that she saw it too. "It helps your eye pull everything together."

"Even so," she replied, getting back on the subject. "You have to embrace the fact that you're a seventh grader. Middle school has to be enough, because that's your full-time job. That's your life. So, you can either run for student council tomorrow. Or I can have your mom come down here and start giving you pep talks about how 'seventh grade will be seventh heaven' and why you 'need to be your true self.'"

"You'd never do that to me," I said.

She gave me a sly smile and said, "I think you know me well enough to know that's exactly what I'd do."

"Fine," I said in full surrender. "Anything but that."

"So you're telling me you'll run?"

"Yes," I answered reluctantly, trying to convince myself at the same time. "If you say it's great, then it must be great."

The next day Jennifer Damon and I were elected to be the student council representatives for Mr. White's homeroom. Three other girls ran, and I think I squeaked in because they split the popular-girl vote, thereby leaving the geeky-boy superhero-fan-club constituency all for me.

Slowly but surely, I was taking baby steps into accepting my middle school–ness.

When I woke up Saturday morning, it had been twelve days since I'd left Ford's Theatre. Twelve days with no connection to the mystery. Twelve days for my mind to reboot, just like they rebooted the security system at the National Gallery.

That's when I had my revelation.

Maybe I needed those twelve days off because, when I finally saw it, it seemed as clear as day. And I marched right across the street to Margaret's house to tell her all about it.

"We have betrayed our core beliefs!" I exclaimed when she answered the door. "I have just had an epic realization."

I blustered into her house, only to stop when I saw myself in a hallway mirror. "This is what it's like to be you, isn't it?" I said. "This is what it's like to burst into a room half-way through a conversation that the other person didn't even know had started."

She looked at me and shook her head in total confusion. "I have absolutely no idea what you're talking about."

"Ha!" I said, pointing at her. "And that's what it's like to be me. I never know either. You get used to it."

"How have we betrayed our core beliefs?"

"By ignoring TOAST," I told her. "What is it? Give me your best definition."

"Okay," she said, getting into the spirit of it. "The Theory of All Small Things ignores the seemingly obvious to consider only small details so that when they're added together they reveal an undeniable truth."

I stopped and smiled. "That's a really good way to put it."

"Thanks, I may have practiced it in my head a couple thousand times. You know . . . because I'm me."

"Unfortunately, that's not what we've been doing," I said. "We haven't been ignoring the obvious to focus on the details. We've only been looking for the details that make the big things more likely to seem true."

"I think you may have lost me for part of that," she said.

"I know. I'm not expressing it nearly as well as you, but I think we've been looking at this all wrong. I think we need to go back to playing TOAST again. That's how we got as far as we did."

She looked at me as she considered this before finally saying, "Okay. Where do you want to play?"

I did not hesitate with my answer. "The Romanian embassy."

"You can't be serious," she said. "Agent Rivers specifically said that you couldn't go near there. It's against the law."

"No," I corrected. "He said that the FBI couldn't investigate there. And when it comes to this case, I no longer have anything to do with the FBI. I am a civilian. The Romanian embassy is holding an open house to share its culture with the people of Washington. That's us."

"Really?" she asked. "This is what you want to do?"

"When will we ever get a chance to look at Nevrescu using TOAST?" I said. "This is our one shot. He'll be there schmoozing and mingling and we'll be able to see him in action. And we're the only ones who can do it. The FBI can't go in. Only we can find these clues. Only we can ignore the version of him that's in the papers, and look for the little details that will tell us the truth."

"And what if he recognizes you?"

"He won't," I said confidently. "It was just a coincidence that we both were at your soccer game."

"Why do I have a feeling that if I don't agree to go, you're going to go without me?"

"Because you're smart and that's exactly what I'm going to do."

"Okay, then I'll do it," she said. "Just let me get my sneakers. You know, in case we end up having to run out of there."

A few minutes later we were on our way.

I used cash to ride the Metro because I'd purposely left my SmarTrip card home. I didn't want any alarms to let Agent Rivers know what I was doing. We got off at the Dupont Circle station and walked up Massachusetts Avenue for about half a mile.

"There it is," I said, pointing across the street as we neared the embassy.

The building was three stories tall and had a massive antenna on the roof. The front doors were open and the sound of music could be heard from inside.

"Once we set foot on the driveway, we're no longer in America," I reminded her as we crossed the street. "So let's make sure we don't do anything stupid."

"Good tip," she said. "I don't suppose you memorized any of those Romanian phrases?"

"Just one."

"Let me guess," she replied. "My hovercraft is full of monkeys."

"That's the one."

We walked along the circular driveway until we reached the front door, where a bearlike man with a huge smile and a booming voice greeted us. *"Bine ati venit."*

I smiled back at him and said, *"Multumesc."*

"What just happened there?" Margaret asked once we stepped inside the entryway, where there was a grand staircase.

"He said, 'Welcome,' and I said, 'Thank you,'" I explained.

"I thought you didn't speak Romanian," she said.

"I don't," I answered. "But I can fake a little here and there. Like I said, it's similar to Italian."

The festival was limited to the bottom floor, and while most of the rooms were open to the public, they were very specific about not going into any rooms with closed doors. In one room a violinist performed traditional folk music, while in another a stereo pulsated with Romanian dance pop. And everywhere we went, there was food.

"You have got to try these cabbage rolls," Margaret told me in between bites. "De-licious."

"Do you see any sign of Nevrescu?" I asked.

"No," she said. "But I can take a look over there by that table full of fried dough and sweet cheese."

A pattern quickly emerged as we went from room to room. Wherever we'd go, I'd look for Nevrescu, and Margaret would look for food. Her search had a much better success rate than mine until we reached the library.

The room was beautiful with antique furniture and dark wood bookcases that went from floor to ceiling. It was packed with people and I spied Nevrescu in the opposite corner doing the meet and greet with everyone.

"There he is," I said, nodding toward him.

"Excellent," mumbled Margaret as she finished swallowing a dessert known as *papanash*. "And with 'excellent' I'm referring to both the fact that you found Nevrescu and this dessert. OMG, it's delicious."

Nic the Knife's social swirl seemed to stay in that particular area, so I found a spot where we were somewhat shielded from his view by a large cabinet.

"If he has no idea who you are, then why are you hiding?" she asked.

I didn't really have an answer for that one, so all I did was smile.

"That's what I thought," she said.

Then I pulled out a pair of glasses and put them on.

"What are those?" asked Margaret.

"Glasses," I answered as if it were beyond obvious.

"Yes, but you don't wear glasses," she said. "So I repeat, 'what are those?'"

"Okay," I whispered. "Maybe they're spy glasses with a built-in camera that Agent Rivers gave me at Quantico."

She shook her head and let out a sigh of resignation. "I can tell this is going to turn out really well."

"All we're doing is playing TOAST," I reminded her. "The glasses are so we can go back to the instant replay if we need to. All systems are go."

Seeing Nevrescu in action completely changed my perception of him. Despite the intense death stare that was on display in all the photos we came across, in person he seemed charming, even from a distance. For example, when he'd meet someone, he'd always make sure to shake with one hand, and clasp them on the arm with the other. It was friendly and warm. And definitely not what I expected. We watched him for about fifteen minutes, making sure he never caught sight of us.

The plan worked really well until I saw someone totally unexpected. There was a swinging door that led to the kitchen and when it opened I got a quick glimpse of a man loading a trash can. The door swung shut again before I could be certain, but he seemed to be wearing the same blue coveralls as the custodians who worked at the National Gallery.

"Did you see that?" I asked Margaret.

"Did I see what?"

I headed for the kitchen and pressed the door just enough to look inside.

"Florian, where are you going?" asked Margaret, a hint of desperation in her voice.

"I just want to take a peek," I said, pushing it more.

"They were pretty specific about where we could and couldn't go," she reminded me. "The key detail was that closed doors were a no-go."

I pushed the door all the way open and said, "But this door isn't closed anymore."

"Why are boys always this way?" she said, shaking her head.

I didn't stay to answer. I looked into the kitchen, and when I saw that no one was in there, I went all the way in. The only way I was going to get a decent look was to go into the next room.

"And now he's totally gone off the deep end," I heard Margaret say as the door swung shut behind me.

I don't know what came over me, but I wasn't scared in the least. I was determined to find him. I strode right across the kitchen and entered a pantry . . . where two security guards were taking a cigarette break.

"What's this?" demanded one of the guards.

I stammered for a moment and failed miserably as I tried to use the Romanian phrase for "where is the bathroom?" I can't be certain but I'm pretty sure I asked for the hovercraft.

"Speak in English," said the other guard.

"Oh, great, you speak English," I replied, my brain a total blank as to what to say. "That means I can speak in English to you."

I was still stammering away when a voice called out from behind.

"Johan, what are you doing?"

Agent Rivers had come to my rescue. He was dressed kind of nerdy in a plaid shirt with a name tag that read, MR. MIKE EVANS, NORTH BETHESDA MIDDLE SCHOOL. And when he talked, his voice had an excitable quality to it.

"I'm so sorry," he said to the guards. "My name's Mike Evans. I'm the art teacher at North Bethesda Middle. Go Firebirds! Anyway, I brought two of my best students here to fully immerse themselves in the culture of another country. Unfortunately, Johan here has a tendency to wander off where he shouldn't. What have I told you about that, Johan?"

"Not to do it," I said, still totally confused as to how he got here but so grateful that he did.

"Anyway, I was led to believe that there would be a display of traditional Romanian painted eggs that we could look at. As an artist, I feel they truly capture the spirit and heritage of your country. I'd really like to show my students those eggs because next month we're going to be painting similar ones in class, and I think yours would give them an excellent target, creatively speaking. They are just exquisite."

By the time he stopped talking long enough to take a breath, the guards had practically forgotten about me and were just looking to get back to their cigarettes.

"So can you tell me where they are?" Rivers asked.

"Where what are?" one guard asked, confused.

"The eggs. The painted Romanian eggs. I'd like to show them to the students."

"Fine, fine," he replied. "The eggs are in the library. But no more wandering, okay?"

All eyes turned to me.

"I promise," I said.

We left the kitchen and beelined for the front door.

"How'd you know I was here?" I asked under my breath once we'd gotten clear of the guards.

"Johan Blankvort sent a message to 'Ask an Agent' wanting to know 'Where is the Embassy of Romania?' An odd question for an FBI agent, but certainly one that caught my attention."

"But I didn't send in any question," I said, even more confused.

"That was me," said Margaret. "When I went to get my sneakers."

"You went behind my back?"

"No, she saved your butt," Rivers corrected. "Although, it may be short-lived because there's a decent chance I'm going to kill you when we get out of here."

We made it to the entryway and were almost to the grand staircase when I saw Nicolae Nevrescu talking to a young woman in a blue dress. He seemed to be flirting with her. Right up until the point he looked our way.

"Um, we may have a problem."

When I saw Nevrescu signal a humongous bodyguard to come over to him, I corrected that statement.

"Oh yeah, we definitely have a problem."

25.

The Getaway

MARGARET, AGENT RIVERS, AND I WERE ABOUT twenty-five feet from the front door when Nicolae Nevrescu saw me. The look of recognition and surprise on his face was unmistakable. And worst of all, there was no way I could beat him to the door.

"He knows me," I said under my breath to Rivers. "He just spotted me."

"He may know you," said Marcus, "but he doesn't know me. You two do not stop walking until you make it to the sidewalk. Kayla's waiting for you."

"Kayla who taught me self-defense at Quantico?"

"She'll be off to the right when you get through the door,"

he said. "She's standing on the line that marks the end of their jurisdiction. Do not stop walking until you reach her."

Now Nevrescu was headed right to us, but there was no way to know if he could tell that Rivers was with us or not.

"What about you?" I asked Rivers nervously. "What are you going to do?"

He didn't answer. Instead he just resumed playing the role of the very excitable middle school teacher.

"Mr. Nevrescu," he said as he cut him off and blocked him from reaching us. "My name is Mike Evans and I'm the art teacher at North Bethesda Middle. I just want to say that I am a huge fan of your scholarship program. I just think it's amazing that you've helped so many deserving kids."

He kept talking but I could no longer make out what he was saying once we got to the door.

"Go, go, go," said Margaret as she took me by the arm and hurried me along.

I turned to look back over my shoulder but couldn't see Rivers in the crush of people and had no way of knowing if his act was working or if things were going to go very wrong for him. Margaret kept pulling me along.

Then another voice called out, "Wait one second. Come back."

It was the bodyguard Nevrescu had signaled inside the

embassy. He was about six foot six, so his strides were long and he was catching up.

"Sorry," I called back to him, picking up the pace. "But we're running late."

I looked to the right and saw Kayla, all bright and smiley. She had on jeans, a tank top, and a pair of boots that maybe nudged her over the five-foot mark.

"There's our rescue team," I told Margaret.

"Seriously?" she replied uneasily. "The kindergarten teacher?"

"Don't be fooled," I assured her.

"Come back or else," the bodyguard demanded as he closed the gap some more.

Kayla was careful to stay beyond the sidewalk, but she reached out and signaled us to hurry. "Come on, you two," she said in her cheery voice. "Right over here."

We reached her just as the bodyguard reached us, and she swept us with her arm so that we were directly behind her.

"You two need to come back," he said, ignoring her. "It's important."

"Actually," Kayla said. "They don't need to do anything. You see, they're with me."

The man laughed. "And who are you? Their babysitter?"

"You know, I did babysit back home in Pennsylvania," she said as she took his hand. It looked as if she was going to shake it, but instead she started to twist his pinkie and ring fingers and practically brought him to his knees. "But today I'm not a babysitter. Today I'm your worst nightmare."

The amazing thing was that even as she was physically destroying and taunting him, she kept talking in that upbeat kindergarten teacher's voice. She continued to twist his fingers and he grimaced in agony, a line of sweat forming on his forehead.

"Now, I'm wearing my favorite boots," she continued. "And I don't want to mess them up. But if you so much as make another move toward either of these children, I will not hesitate to use them in ways that you will find excruciatingly uncomfortable."

Just then a black SUV pulled up next to us.

"You two get in," Kayla instructed us without turning her attention from the bodyguard.

I opened the door and we both jumped in. Once we were safely inside, Kayla finished her conversation with the man.

"So do we understand each other?"

He didn't respond at first, which caused her to twist the fingers even more.

"Yes," he said. "We understand each other."

She flashed a smile and said, "It was a pleasure to meet you."

She let go and he pulled back his injured hand and clutched it with the other. Kayla literally had to jump up to get into the backseat with us. Once she did, she slammed the door shut, the power locks closed, and the SUV was moving down Massachusetts Avenue.

She looked over at Margaret and smiled. "Hey, I'm Kayla."

"Hi," Margaret said. "You're my hero."

Kayla laughed. "You'd be surprised, but I get that a lot."

As we drove away, I turned around in my seat so I could look out the rear window to see if Agent Rivers had made it out of the embassy. I didn't see any sign of him.

"We have a covert asset," Kayla instructed the agent behind the wheel. "Drive accordingly."

"Roger that," said the driver as he picked up the pace.

We stayed on Massachusetts Avenue, which is also known as Embassy Row, for about a mile. Then we started making some sudden turns onto little side roads. I could feel car sickness coming on.

"He's just making sure no one's following," explained Kayla.

"That's good," I said. "That man you destroyed. Is he going to cause trouble for you?"

She laughed. "He is going to go to his grave without admitting to anybody that he was outmuscled by little ol' me."

Margaret laughed.

Kayla looked at me and shook her head. "Florian, what were you thinking?"

"I don't know," I admitted.

"You are unbelievably smart," she said. "This was anything but."

"I know."

That was the entire lecture I got from her, but I was certain there were more to come.

"Are we clear?" she asked the driver.

"Absolutely," he replied. "No one's following."

"Great, take us to the Washington Field Office.

"I'm stationed there and not at the Hoover," she said to me.

"I'm worried about Agent Rivers," I said. "I didn't see him come out of the embassy."

"Yeah, well, he was sure worried about you," she replied. "Thank goodness you had enough sense to send a distress signal."

"Actually that was Margaret," I said. "Thanks, Margaret."

"It's okay," she said. "That's what BFs do, right?"

Ten minutes later we pulled into the underground garage

at the FBI Washington Field Office. It was large and nondescript, about a half mile from the Hoover Building. A few minutes after we got there, another car pulled up beside us. It was a maroon hybrid. Agent Rivers was behind the wheel.

I let out a huge sigh of relief.

"Looks like your ride is here," she said. "So it's time for me to say good-bye. You two stay out of trouble, okay?"

"Okay," I said.

"Definitely," said Margaret.

"And, Florian," she said, looking me right in the eyes. "That big brain of yours . . . don't forget to use it."

We got out of the SUV and Agent Rivers came right to me.

"Florian, I can't believe you did that," he said. "I am so angry with you."

"I know," I replied.

"But we are going to deal with the anger a little later," he said.

That's when he wrapped me up in a hug. It was tight and comforting and long.

"I'm sorry, Agent Rivers," I said, looking up at him.

"You call me Marcus."

I nodded. "I'm sorry, Marcus."

26.

Black Tuesday

"EPIC" IS ONE OF MARGARET'S FAVORITE WORDS. It's also a good way to describe the scope of the grounding my parents gave me after Agent Rivers drove us home and told them what happened.

I made a point of explaining to Margaret's mom and dad how I'd put her in an impossible situation. And Marcus followed up by pointing out that she was the one who saved the day, so we were able to help her a little. But my world was limited to the campus of Alice Deal Middle School and the walls of my house for as far as the eye could see. And while at home, the computer was limited only to its role in helping with homework, and the television was banished as though Philo T. Farnsworth had never invented it.

And I totally deserved the punishment. Every bit of it.

The one exception was that I was allowed to keep participating in after-school activities. Suddenly I became the most active member in student council history, volunteering for any subcommittee or planning board I could get on.

Two weeks after our little adventure to Romania, I came out of an oversight committee that considered possible changes in the school dress code—like I said, I volunteered for *everything*—and was surprised to see my dad waiting for me in front of the school.

"What's wrong? Mom's worried I'm having too much fun on my walk home?" I joked as I got in the car.

"Worse," he said, a serious look on his face. "There's been a new development. The story broke. All of it. A writer at the *Post* published it online about two hours ago. TV news jumped on board and now it's a circus."

"I don't understand—what story?"

"They're reporting that *Woman with a Parasol* was stolen, and claiming the FBI and National Gallery kept it a secret out of embarrassment. Nicolae Nevrescu was identified as the prime suspect." He turned to look at me. "And there've been mentions that a boy has been part of the investigation."

"Did they use my name?"

"Not yet," he said. "But there are so many bigger parts of the story right now. It's really going to cause problems for Agent Rivers."

"It'll put pressure on Nevrescu, too," I said.

"One of the news stations ambushed him outside his construction company," said Dad. "There was a lot of shouting and yelling."

When I got home the television and computer bans were temporarily lifted so that we could watch the story unfold. Margaret came over and joined Dad and me.

"How'd the story even get out?" I asked as we watched a reporter do a live update from the sidewalk in front of the museum.

"It's like I told you," Margaret replied. "Nothing stays secret in Washington."

As far as names, the only ones mentioned much were Marcus Rivers as the agent in charge and Nicolae Nevrescu as the prime suspect. A few reporters revealed that there may have been involvement in the crime by museum staff, but no one referred directly to Serena Miller or Earl Jackson.

Oliver Hobbes, however, was all over the news. Not as a suspect but as someone to be interviewed. We saw him on two national broadcasts as an industry expert with a working knowledge of the situation.

"I bet he's your leak right there," said Dad.

"Oliver?"

"He's always had a shady side."

"But why would he leak the story?" asked Margaret.

"I'm sure he's getting pressure from the insurance company," Dad said. "They probably think the FBI is moving too slowly and wanted to put them in the hot seat."

"My company was against keeping the theft a secret right from the beginning," Hobbes said during his interview. "We believe that the best policy is total honesty with the public. But the FBI insisted and we were forced into silence."

"That's pretty harsh," interjected Margaret.

"And why do you think the FBI kept it a secret?" asked the interviewer.

"Isn't it obvious?" said Hobbes. "They don't want the public to know how much they've messed up."

When Mom got home from work, she gave us a behind-the-scenes account of the National Gallery.

"Everyone was running around crazy," she said. "Reporters kept trying to come inside with their television crews. Serena Miller went in for a closed-door meeting with the director that lasted over an hour. Eventually my boss came into our studio and told us to leave early and not speak to the press."

"Does anyone there know that you already knew?"

Mom shook her head. "I'm good at keeping secrets. I played dumb like everybody else."

As far as my participation, a few reporters mentioned a rumor about a kid being involved, but it seemed so far-fetched and strange that no one gave it much thought. I had my fingers crossed that things would stay that way.

"Wait a second," said Margaret, holding her hands up to signal stop. "Where's Pavel Novak?"

"In the Czech Republic," I said, unsure what she was going for.

"No, I don't mean where is he on the planet. I mean, where is he in the story?" she asked. "He's the one person that we definitely know is involved in the crime, and no one has mentioned his name."

"That's true," I said.

"They must not know," said Dad. "Whoever leaked the story must not know about Novak's involvement."

"Then it's not Hobbes," I said. "He's known from the beginning."

"Then who could it be?" Margaret asked, thinking out loud.

"Oh no," said Mom. "This does not look good."

We looked over to her and she was glued to the monitor.

"What's the matter?" I asked.

"Marcus is in trouble."

We all quieted and turned up the volume and listened as a news anchor held up a piece of paper and began to read from it.

"According to this statement from Nevrescu's attorney, the businessman categorically denies any involvement," she said. "In a troubling twist, there are reports Special Agent Marcus Rivers may have entered the Romanian embassy under a false identity two weeks ago."

The anchor next to her shook his head as though this was an earth-shattering development. "If that's true, it would be a clear violation of international law," said the anchor. "I'm sure the State Department will be getting involved now."

I couldn't believe it. On top of everything else, Marcus was going to get in trouble because of something I did. It was my fault and he was going to pay the price.

"They're going to fire him, aren't they?" I said. "It's going to cost him his career."

"You may be right," said Dad.

Then Mom reached over and put her hand on my shoulder. "Unless you solve it first."

"Seriously?" I said.

Mom and Dad shared a look for a moment and then both of them turned to me. "There is a temporary lifting of the restriction within the confines of the Underground. Just downstairs. You can't talk to anyone. You can't go anywhere."

"We don't need to go anywhere. The TV's bringing it all to us." I looked right at Margaret. "This is our test. Are you ready?"

"Ready to take it. Ready to crush it."

27.

Kidnapped

MARGARET AND I SPENT TUESDAY EVENING AND
all day after school Wednesday in the Underground trying
to break the case. We were in total TOAST mode, ignoring
the big things to focus on little details that didn't quite fit.

Here were some of the things we wanted to figure out:

1. Who leaked the story? We filled an entire
   wall with cards that listed who knew what
   and when. Then we started comparing those
   names with what information did and did not
   become public.

2. What was the importance of the cleaning crew? When we looked back at the video my secret-agent glasses recorded at the Romanian embassy, we were able to identify that the custodian there worked for the same company as the custodians at the National Gallery.

3. How did the burglar find out about the security upgrade? If neither Serena nor Earl was involved—which we believed in our hearts to be true—then someone else had to pass along the information about the upgrade. Who could have known about it?

4. Who else crossed paths with Pavel Novak?

"Okay," Margaret said, staring at the evidence on the wall. "I've got one more for you. But I warn you, it's really TOASTy."

"What does 'really TOASTy' mean?" I asked.

"I mean in the Theory of All Small Things, this is smaller than small. It's tiny. But it doesn't make sense," she explained.

"Lay it on me," I said.

"How'd he know about the soccer game?"

She just let it sit there for a moment.

"What do you mean?"

"We know there's a Romanian connection."

"Right."

"And it all points to Nevrescu as the mastermind."

"Yes, but we can't prove it."

"Nevrescu recognized you at the embassy because he had seen you at the soccer game."

"Right," I said.

"But how did he know you would be at the soccer game in the first place? He didn't follow you from your house. The FBI would have mentioned that. But they just said he went to the soccer game and watched you there."

I considered this and smiled.

"You're absolutely right," I said. "It's tiny, but that may be the piece."

That question kept me up all night and bothered me all through the next school day. How could Nevrescu have known where I was going?

"Your SmarTrip card!" Margaret said the instant she saw me in the cafeteria on Thursday. "The agent knew you were there because your SmarTrip card set off some kind of alarm. Nevrescu must have access to the same information or equipment."

I thought this through for a minute. "You might be right. But that would mean he has some sort of connection inside the FBI. We've got to reach out to Marcus."

"He can't talk to you," she said. "He's all over the news. I'm sure he's in the admiral's office fighting for his job. You can't just have Johan Blankvort send a question into 'Ask an Agent.'"

"Well, we've got to do something," I said. "Let's go straight to my house after school."

"I can't. I have my piano lesson."

"Oh yeah, I forgot," I told her. "I'll run home and start trying to figure out a connection between Nevrescu and the FBI. You come over as soon as you can."

"Okay, and I know you're in a hurry. But don't take all your little shortcuts."

"What's wrong with my shortcuts?"

"Like the one behind the Safeway. It's gross back there. And you know what I say about Dumpsters."

"You don't have to worry about me," I said. "You just get to the Underground as soon as you can."

It was pouring when school got out, and I tried to reach both of my parents to see if either could pick me up. They couldn't, so I decided to run through the rain, and despite Margaret's warnings, I planned to take every shortcut I knew.

I ran down the street and squeezed between the fence to get behind the Safeway. I held my backpack over my head to try to keep dry as I hurried along the Dumpsters.

And that brings the story back to where I started—my kidnapping. A lot has happened since then, so I'll recap some of the highlights.

The giant man from the Happy Leprechaun Flower Shop knocked me unconscious, threw me into the back of the truck, and drove me to a farm in rural Virginia. Along the way we semibonded over the joke about monkeys in my hovercraft, and then I was able to trick him into triggering my panic button, which was disguised as an asthma inhaler.

Oh, and I was seated at a table across from Nicolae Nevrescu, crime lord and art-theft mastermind.

"You are the one the FBI only talks about in whispers. The one they call Little Sherlock," he said.

"I have no idea what you're talking about," I said.

He gave me a disappointed look. "Let's not play games. I know who you are and you know who I am."

I nodded reluctantly. "I know you're the man who master-minded the robbery at the National Gallery of Art."

He chuckled. "Mastermind? I love that word. I wish it were true. No, that fact you have wrong. That's why I had you brought here. So we could set the record straight and you could tell your friends at the FBI they are looking for the wrong suspect."

That's when he rolled up his sleeves and I saw the tattoos. The one that caught my eye was the tattoo of the daisy with the numbers "24/7" directly beneath it. Nothing about that made sense. It just didn't fit.

Until it did. Until it answered Margaret's question: How did he know I'd be at the soccer game?

"There's been a huge mistake," I said urgently. "You need to let me go right now."

"Is that so?" He laughed. "Why should I do that?"

I looked right at him and did not blink. "Because the FBI is going to be here in less than five minutes and that doesn't leave us much time to talk about why your tattoo changes everything."

This caught him off guard.

"That inhaler," I said. "That's really a panic button. The FBI has been alerted and they are going to come crashing through the door. And we have to talk about your tattoo before that happens, don't we?"

His eyes narrowed and his lips tightened. And then he answered, "Yes, we do."

Nevrescu barked at everybody else, telling them to leave as he untied my hands. Both of us had to think fast. As the others scurried out of the barn and rushed to their vehicles, Nevrescu and I sat back down.

"How did you know?" he asked.

"Your tattoo doesn't make sense. You're a tough guy, not a flower guy. Then I remembered the Romanian word for daisy—*margareta*, MARGARET A. The twenty-four/seven is the European style for the twenty-fourth of July. That's her real birthday, right? July twenty-fourth?"

I looked across the table and saw him turn into an entirely different man.

"You're Margaret's father."

28.

The Cavalry Arrives

THE FBI WAS COMING TO RESCUE ME, NEVRESCU'S henchmen were scrambling to get away from the barn, chaos was everywhere, but I didn't hear a thing. I was so focused on Nevrescu's tattoo and the realization that he was Margaret's birth father.

"You weren't at the soccer game to see *me*," I said. "You were there to see *her*."

"She was amazing in that game, wasn't she?" he said.

"She's amazing in everything she does," I told him.

I ran through the timeline in my head. "And when we were at the embassy, I wasn't the one you recognized, it was her. She was standing right next to me."

"You must understand that I'm a bad person," he said. "But she is not. She is only good. Nothing can ever connect her to me. That's for her safety."

All the pieces started coming together.

"Twelve years ago, you weren't a criminal, you were a student at Georgetown. Is that where you met her mother, her birth mother?"

"My family would not accept the relationship. They would not accept an African-American daughter-in-law, an African-American granddaughter. So I had to make a choice. I had to become this man, in exchange for my family looking away from them. I tell you this so you understand how far I will go to protect Margaret. You cannot tell anyone."

"Well, then you're going to have to help me come up with an explanation as to what we're doing here," I said. "Because the FBI's going to want to know how we ended up together."

Both of us sat there for a moment, breathing heavily, trying to figure out a solution. I knew the FBI would be there any moment. I pictured my case board in my mind and I drew a line through all the dots. I connected all the small pieces, and then I saw it.

"I know who did it!" I exclaimed. "I know who stole *Woman with a Parasol*!"

"It was not me," he said.

"No, it wasn't," I said. "You had nothing to do with it. That's how I know who did it."

We could now hear cars arriving outside the barn. It was only a matter of seconds before the agents burst into the barn.

"You can help me in a way that will help both of us."

Nevrescu lay facedown on the ground and put his hands behind his head, so there'd be no trouble when the agents entered.

"What do I do?" he asked.

"You get EEL to force Pavel Novak to return to America," I said. "And you tell everybody that Agent Rivers was not the man at the Romanian embassy. Tell them that you saw a man who looked like him, but that it was someone else. That one's a deal breaker. You don't do that and I'll tell everybody everything. Including Margaret."

"You care about her too much to tell her," he said. "But I still agree."

The barn door flew open and a team of federal agents burst in. They wore black riot gear and helmets and had their guns drawn. It was terrifying. In the middle of them all was Agent Rivers.

"Nicolae Nevrescu, keep your hands behind your head and do not move!" he barked as an agent approached Nevrescu and cuffed him behind his back.

Rivers walked straight to me.

"Are you okay?" he said.

"Don't worry, Marcus, I'm fine."

He wrapped me in another hug.

"This is going to have to stop," he said with a nervous laugh. "I signed up for Art Crime because it was supposed to keep me mellow."

"Yeah," I agreed. "But we've got a lot to talk about."

After the dust settled (literally) and the scene had been fully secured by the agents, Nicolae, Marcus, and I were all seated around the wooden picnic table, only now it was Nic the Knife, whose hands were tied behind his back.

"You're telling me that it was all a misunderstanding?" Rivers asked incredulously after we'd started to fill him in on our version of events.

"Not all of it," Nicolae said. "I asked Gregor to get Florian so that I could help explain that I was innocent but willing to help solve the mystery. Gregor mistook the request and was too forceful in the manner in which he got Florian. But he was never in danger. This is a special boy and I would not let anything happen to him." He looked at me and added, "I *will* not let anything ever happen to him."

I realized that he meant what he was saying. I was important to Margaret; he would never have hurt her by hurting me.

"But the important thing is that we solved the mystery," I said. "We know who stole *Woman with a Parasol*, and Nicolae can help us get Pavel Novak."

"Of course," Nic said. "I have friends in the Czech Republic who owe me a favor. Novak will be on a plane to the United States within three days. I guarantee that he'll surrender to the authorities."

"You know who did it?" Rivers asked me.

I nodded.

"Who?"

"I'll tell you when we're alone, but there's one more thing we have to take care of."

"What's that?"

"Nicolae, do you know this man?" I asked as I pointed at Agent Rivers. "Did you see him two Saturdays ago at the Romanian embassy?"

Nevrescu gave a performance worthy of an Oscar as he said, "I have never seen this man before in my life. And I would testify to that in any court in the land."

29.

A Tiny Piece of TOAST

MARCUS AND I RODE ALONG THE HIGHWAY ON our way back to Washington. I was still overwhelmed by everything as I looked out at the farms.

"It's a lot prettier when you're not tied up in the back of a truck," I said.

"Funny how that works," he replied.

"I still can't believe I pushed my panic button and you came to rescue me in a *hybrid*. I was expecting something like a helicopter, or at least one of those bulletproof SUVs."

"I didn't come because of the panic button," he said.

"What do you mean?"

"When you didn't show up at home, I started looking

for you on my own, tracking you with your SmarTrip card," he explained. "You got everybody else when you pushed the panic button. I was already on my way."

"I bet you didn't even go over the speed limit," I said.

"Speed limits are there for a reason," he said. "Safety's important." Then he cracked a smile and added, "Although I may have gone over it, by like forty miles an hour."

"Well, thanks," I said. "You've rescued me twice in two weeks. That's got to be some sort of record."

"And you said you were going to tell me who did it," he reminded me. "So spill."

"I need to explain something first. And you have to promise that you won't tell anyone."

"I promise no such thing," he said.

"Forty-five minutes ago, I told a very scary man that I wouldn't tell this to anybody, so I need to make sure it stays a secret. You have to promise."

"Let me explain how this works," Marcus said to me. "If you trust me with a secret, that means you trust my judgment with regard to the information. Not that you get to dictate that judgment for me. If we're going to work together, we're going to have to be able to think along those lines."

"You still want to work with me?" I asked. "Even after all this?"

"I know, crazy, isn't it?"

"Okay, you don't have to promise, but please use your best judgment."

"Always," he said.

"It all starts with Margaret's soccer game . . ."

I explained to him all about the search for Margaret's birth parents and the fact that Nevrescu was her father. When I was done he shook his head in amazement.

"Wow," he said. "That's a secret I can keep. That's something we need to protect her from."

"Agreed," I said.

"And from that you were able to determine who stole *Woman with a Parasol*?"

"Yes, thanks to you."

"What did I do?"

"That day at Quantico you set a trap for me."

I reached into the glove compartment and saw that the nail polish was still there. I took it out and held it up for him to see.

"You left clues like this that were too irresistible for me to ignore," I said. "Then you told me that my biggest vulnerability was that if someone knew I was on a case, they could set a trap. And that's exactly what someone did."

We continued to drive as I laid it all out for him. . . .

30.

The Solution

I WON'T GET INTO ALL THE MUSHY DETAILS, BUT IT was pretty emotional when I got home. At one point I think my mother literally hugged me for thirty consecutive minutes without letting go. After repeated assurances that I was completely fine, she slowly loosened her grip long enough so that we could eat dinner.

Afterward Margaret came over and we all sat around the front room and ate rocky road ice cream. That's when I got the text from Marcus.

"What?" asked Margaret when she saw my grin.

"The case is closed," I declared triumphantly.

"How?" asked Mom.

"Did I forget to tell you guys the part where I figured out who stole *Woman with a Parasol*?"

"Yes!" exclaimed Margaret.

"Well, I wanted to wait to make sure I was right," I said. "And apparently I was, because he's about to make an arrest."

"Who is it?" asked Dad.

"Let's turn on the TV, so we can see the press conference," I said.

When I turned it on, Oliver Hobbes was on yet another talk show complaining about the FBI and National Gallery. "It's almost criminal that such cultural treasures are protected so poorly," he said.

"Ugh," said my mom. "I cannot listen to that man say another word. Please shut him up."

"Okay," I said, pressing the mute button.

"Now tell us everything," added Margaret. "How did you solve it?"

"By answering your question," I told her. "How did Nic the Knife know that I'd be at the soccer game? And the answer is, he didn't."

"What do you mean?" asked Dad.

"He didn't know I'd be there because he didn't care," I said. "It turns out the FBI was wrong about one thing. He did have a relative playing in the game. Some girl on the

Capitol Crush was a second niece or something. He was there to see her, not me."

"Then why did he kidnap you?" asked my mother.

"Because he wanted to explain it to me, so that I could explain it to the FBI," I continued. "You see, once we suspected him, we tried to make the clues fit our suspicions. He kept intersecting the case. Clues kept pointing to him. But once you realize that he's not involved, then those clues disappear. All except for one."

"The auction bids," said Margaret. "Those all pointed back to Romania."

"Yes, they did," I replied. "And that was the final piece of TOAST. If Nevrescu is innocent, that means the bids are fake. They have to be. It's the only solution that works."

"It's Oliver Hobbes!" said Margaret.

I smiled. "You got it. He needed to pin it on somebody, and when Nic the Knife came onto the scene he had the perfect culprit. Nic was already making himself look guilty. All Oliver needed to do was set him up just a little bit more. Since the bidding records he showed us were confidential, he knew we'd never be able to compare them to the originals. All he had to do was leave the clues for us to find."

"And once you figured that out . . ." said Margaret.

"Everything else fell into place," I said. "When we were looking for an insider, we assumed that meant an employee of the museum, so we didn't consider him. But as the insurance representative, he knew exactly when the upgrade was going to take place."

"What about ArtFest in Budapest?" asked Margaret.

"He was there too," I said. "Marcus confirmed it with someone at Interpol. And, Dad, remember how fast you drove to the museum the night the paintings were stolen?"

Mom shot him a look. "Not too fast," he said. "But it was an emergency."

"But when we got to the security center, Oliver was already there on the telephone," I pointed out. "How could he beat us? He lives just down the street from us."

"He was already nearby waiting for the call," said Dad.

"You got it," I said.

"Look at him," Mom said, pointing at Hobbes on the television. "Do you think he has any idea that he's been discovered?"

"No," I said, turning up the volume. "But he's about to."

We watched as Hobbes continued to rant about the FBI, and then in a moment of perfect television, Special Agent Marcus Rivers of the FBI's Art Crime team walked onto the set during the middle of the broadcast.

There were a few seconds of confusion, until the interviewer recognized him.

"Agent Rivers, have you come down here to dispute Mr. Hobbes's claims?" she asked.

"No, I haven't," he said.

"Then why are you here?"

"Just doing my job," he said.

And he arrested Oliver right there on live television. We all cheered. And when it was over, the interviewer tried to switch sides as though she'd always been a supporter.

"Great job," she said, thrusting a microphone into his face. "How did you solve it?"

He looked right into the camera, winked, and said, "No comment."

Two days later Pavel Novak was greeted at Dulles International Airport, where he surrendered to authorities and began talking in exchange for a reduced sentence. He told them that Oliver Hobbes, whom he'd met at ArtFest in Budapest, had approached a Czech crime boss with the idea. Hobbes provided them with the information about the security reset and in return was to receive *Woman with a Parasol*. The Czechs, meanwhile, were supposed to keep the three paintings that we'd discovered in the recycling Dumpster.

Armed with this information, the FBI was able to get

Hobbes to confess. He had dressed up as the extra custodian, and his plan was to sneak the Monet out of the museum in his car that night. But he was too slow and the police had managed to block the scene before he could escape. So instead, he hid the masterpiece in a secured locker that the insurance company maintained at the museum. Like the first three paintings, it never actually ventured outside of the building. It had been so close to us the entire time we were looking for it.

Special Agent Marcus Rivers was hailed as a hero, and despite numerous media requests, he granted only one interview.

It was with *Viking Journal*, the student newspaper at Alice Deal Middle School.

31.

The (Sort Of) Safeway

MY NAME IS FLORIAN BATES. I'M TWELVE YEARS old and a seventh grader at Alice Deal Middle School in Washington, DC. I'm a consulting detective for the FBI, I'm a rabid fan of the DC Dynamo girls soccer team, and I never leave leftover egg rolls for fear that they'd remain uneaten in the event of a zombie apocalypse.

I also helped thwart the biggest art heist in US history.

And nobody knows about it. Well, almost no one.

And that's okay because the people who do know are the only ones that matter to me. My parents, who despite taking too many pictures, are pretty great; my FBI handler, who somehow manages to be cool and geeky, old-school and cutting-edge, all at the same time; and my best friend, who's . . . well . . . who's the best person I've ever known. And it really sucks, because I know the answer to the one question that matters the most to her, and I can't tell her. I have to lie.

But other than that, life's pretty great.

Margaret and I are walking home from school, and I jokingly nod toward the rear of the Safeway.

"What do you say?" I ask. "Want to take a shortcut?"

She gives me a look—that trademark Margaret look—and asks, "Do I have to remind you what Ben Franklin said?"

"Ben Franklin did not say, 'Nothing good ever happens when you're surrounded by Dumpsters.' I guarantee it."

"I'm pretty sure he did," she replies. "I think it was in *Poor Richard's Almanack*."

"Ben Franklin was dead long before the Dumpster was even invented. End of story."

She flashes a big smile and admits, "Maybe. But it's still pretty good advice."

"I cannot argue with that," I say, reflecting back on my recent experiences. "I'd have to rate that as 'very strong' on the advice meter."

"So, what are you going to do now that the case is solved, and you're back to being a lowly seventh grader again?"

"Well, seventh grade does have its perks," I say. "For example, you never get kidnapped in the halls."

"You see, and you didn't like those metal detectors at first, but they keep things safe," she jokes.

"And while Florian Bates Investigations is small, we're hoping to grow," I continue.

"That's right, we still have an open case: Hornet's Nest."

The mention of the search for her birth parents fills me with guilt. "I'm really sorry that I haven't found them yet," I say, and I mean it. "I know I promised but . . ."

"It will take as long as it takes," she says, cutting me off. "If there's one thing I know, it's that you'll find them, Florian. I believe in you. Completely."

I'm tempted to tell her everything on the spot. Best friends are truthful with each other, right? But before I can respond, it starts to rain. And not just a little sprinkle but fully drenching rain. I give her a look, and then I look back toward the Safeway.

"You sure you don't want to take the shortcut?" I ask. "It's the fastest way to someplace dry."

She weighs her options for a moment and nods, streams of water already running down her face. "But let's go around that way," she says, pointing to a slightly different route than I took before.

"We'll call that the 'Sort of' Safe Way," I suggest.

We sprint across the street and I hold up the bottom of the chain link fence so that she can get under it. When she reaches the other side, she does the same for me.

"If we run into any shady characters, remember to unleash the fury of your kung fu," I joke.

We run alongside the line of Dumpsters, trying to use our backpacks to shield us from the rain, and when we turn the corner, we run right up against a black, unmarked van, its engine loudly vibrating, its wipers furiously pumping across the windshield.

"I don't believe it!" I say.

"Oh my God," says Margaret. "What have I done?"

The door slides open, and there he is, a massive smile on his face.

"Haven't you learned your lesson yet?" says Special Agent Marcus Rivers. "It's just like Mark Twain said, 'Nothing good ever happens when you're surrounded by Dumpsters.'"

"That's who said it," says Margaret. "Mark Twain."

"It was not Mark Twain!" I protest. "It was Margaret. Margaret made up that quote. Margaret is who said it."

"Well," he says. "Margaret must be pretty smart because it's good advice."

"Yes, it is. She and I have already agreed to that. Is that

why you did this? You came back here to terrify us so you could make up fake quotes about Dumpsters while we stand in the rain?"

"Actually, no," he says.

"Then what are you doing here?"

"It seems as though we have a situation and we need your help." He turns to look right at Margaret and adds, "Both of you. The admiral sent me. So what do you say? You interested?"

Margaret and I share a look, now totally oblivious to the rain pummeling us. Adventure is calling. Who are we to say no?

Acknowledgments

It does not take a superdetective to uncover the fact that a book is the product of many people's hard work. I would like to thank the ones who helped bring Florian and Margaret's adventure into print. First and foremost are my editor, Fiona Simpson, and publisher, Mara Anastas. They combine kindness, creativity, and enduring patience to make Aladdin an author's dream workplace. Like the master criminals Florian tries to expose, they do their handiwork without leaving fingerprints or clues to their involvement, but trust me when I say that it is extensive and essential.

They are part of a much larger Simon & Schuster team that has been part of my writing career from the very beginning. There I would like to thank Katherine Devendorf, Laura Lyn DiSiena, Sara Berko, Carolyn Swerdloff, Emma Sector, Tara Grieco, Shifa Kapadwala, Michelle Leo,

Candace Greene, Anthony Parisi, Betsy Bloom, and Matt Pantoliano.

Just as Florian has Margaret helping him, I have a professional partner in crime, my agent, Rosemary Stimola. She's the one who warns me not to sneak through the Dumpsters, and she's the one who comes to my rescue when I do it anyway. She's also like Margaret in that she's amazing, funny, and a friend for life.

Besides Fiona, Mara, and Rosemary, perhaps no one else helps my books more than the librarians, media specialists, reading specialists, and teachers who every day fight the battle to get books into the hands of kids. It is noble work, and they are my rock stars. I would especially like to thank the librarians of Texas and Florida, who have been among my biggest supporters.

Finally, I want to thank my family. They are the world to me. They inspire me to write. They make me laugh. They make every single day special. Growing up, I always wanted to be a writer. But even more, I wanted to be a husband and a father. I am eternally blessed in that I get to be all three.

Florian and Margaret are back on the case. This time they're investigating a series of middle-school pranks . . . wait, what? But when the president's daughter is involved, the stakes are high, so it's time for some TOAST!

MIDDLE SCHOOL IS HARD.

Solving cases for the FBI is even harder.

Doing both at the same time, well, that's just crazy.

Trust me, I know. My name's Florian Bates, I'm twelve years old, and along with my best friend, Margaret, I'm a consulting detective for the Bureau's Special Projects Team. We assist the FBI, the same way Sherlock Holmes helped Scotland Yard; only Sherlock never had to close a case *and* write a book report on the same night.

He also didn't have to deal with all the other seventh-grade headaches like locker room bullies, nine o'clock curfews, or figuring out what to wear. All he had to do was put on his coat and deerstalker hat. Instant detective.

Me? It seems like I'm always dressed for the wrong occasion. Like when we had to interrogate a witness while I was still in my soccer uniform. Or the time I was wearing my I'M WITH CHEWBACCA T-shirt and we ended up going undercover at the reception for the French ambassador. (In case you're wondering, "*Que la Force soit avec toi*" is how you say "May the Force be with you" in French.)

So when we arrived at the harbor patrol's maintenance-and-repair yard it shouldn't have been a surprise that I was the only one wearing a double-breasted blazer and herringbone tie. My mistake was that when I dressed for the symphony, I forgot to factor in the possibility of racing down the Potomac in a police boat. (I know, you'd think I'd learn.)

The boat was Marcus's idea. He oversees the Special Projects Team and it was a good plan except for one little detail: None of us actually had access to a boat. That meant we had to borrow one.

Margaret and I waited outside the harbormaster's office while he went in to see if he could get the duty sergeant to help us out. The stench of diesel was overwhelming, engine grease was everywhere, and when I saw my reflection in the window, I noticed my tie was crooked.

"What are you doing?" Margaret asked when she saw me fidget with it.

"Trying to straighten the knot," I explained. "It's a Windsor. It's supposed to be perfectly centered."

She gave me a look. That Margaret "you've got to be kidding me" look. "We're standing on a wharf surrounded by gas and grime and you're worried about your tie being crooked. Why don't you try to relax? No one's going to notice."

"Technically it's not a wharf," I corrected. "We're standing on a *dock*. And the dock is part of a *marina*. A wharf is an entirely different thing."

"Seriously?" she replied, shaking her head. "That's your takeaway from what I just said? Correcting my vocabulary?"

I gave her a sheepish smile and apologized. Then I tried to follow her advice and relax. But it wasn't easy. I'm not that good at relaxing on a normal day when nothing's going on, and this was no normal day. We were in the middle of a missing persons case that was beyond baffling.

That morning we'd boarded a school bus for a field trip to the Kennedy Center for the Performing Arts. At the time, our biggest worry was finding a seat just the right distance from the bullies in back and the chaperones in front. Then one of our classmates disappeared into thin air. That might have been okay if it had been a magic show, but like I said, we were there for the symphony. So it was bad.

Suddenly bullies and chaperones didn't seem like such a big deal. We had a case to solve and we weren't having much luck figuring it out. Each clue seemed to lead us further away from the answer. And now, on top of that, I had an additional obstacle to overcome.

"Can I be honest with you?" I asked Margaret.

"This far into the friendship and you don't know?" she said. "You can always be honest with me. In fact, that's all you can be."

That made me smile.

"Okay, so here's the deal," I replied. "I'm not exactly *comfortable* when it comes to boats."

She gave me a curious look. "What does 'not exactly comfortable' mean?"

"They terrify me," I admitted. "They have ever since I saw that movie about the *Titanic*."

"You know it's at least eighty degrees today," she said. "I'm pretty sure we're not going to run into any icebergs."

"I'm not worried about sinking," I explained. "It's just that I got . . . seasick."

"You got seasick *watching* a movie?"

I nodded reluctantly.

"Were you at least on a boat while you were watching it?"

"No. We were home. I'll skip the vivid details, but we ended up having to rent one of those industrial-sized steam cleaners for the carpet and couch."

My thoughts wafted back to the salami sandwich and jalapeño-flavored tortilla chips that began the day in my lunch bag and I wondered if they would soon be reintroduced to the world.

"Well, you might not have to worry about it," Margaret said, looking through the window into the office. "I think Marcus is striking out in there."

Even though we weren't inside, it wasn't hard to guess what the problem was. The harbor patrol was part of the Metropolitan Police Department and Marcus was with the FBI. Those two groups are very protective of their turf and almost never work well together.

"Think we should help out?"

She asked it like a question, but considering she didn't wait for me to answer before she opened the door and went inside, I didn't really have much of a chance to say no.

The sergeant was big with ruddy skin, chubby cheeks, and a mustache that looked like it belonged on a walrus. He stood behind a counter similar to the check-in desk at a hotel and looked as though his patience was gone.

"But this is an emergency," Marcus said, frustrated.

"You keep saying that," replied the cop. "But I haven't heard a thing about it on my radio." He nodded to the police scanner on his desk.

"That's because we're trying to keep it contained to the Secret Service and the FBI," answered Marcus. "We haven't involved the local police yet."

The sergeant flashed a smug smile. "There, you just said it yourself. You don't want to involve the local police. Well, unfortunately for you, these boats belong to the local police. So have a nice day."

Despite my dread of seasickness, I knew we needed the boat, so I tried to help out.

"What if Frankie was missing?" I asked, interrupting. "You'd want us to look for him, wouldn't you?"

The sergeant turned his attention to me and shot me with a laser stare.

"Or imagine your daughter went camping with her Girl Scout troop and got lost in a national park."

"How do you know about my kids?"

I ignored his question. "How would you feel if the park rangers wouldn't help the police who were trying to rescue her because they were from different agencies? How would you feel if they did to you what you're doing to us right now?"

By this point he was really angry, his fat cheeks turning crimson. "I said, how do you know about my kids?" he demanded.

"The nameplate on your desk says you're Frank Bergen Sr.," I explained. "That means there's a junior. I know you call him Frankie because that's how he signed the drawing you taped to the window over there. I know your daughter's in Girl Scouts because you've got five cases of Girl Scout cookies stacked behind your desk so you can deliver them to your coworkers."

He started to say something, but I just kept talking.

"I don't know your kids at all, but I know you're the kind of dad who tapes his son's pictures up at work and tries to help his daughter sell cookies. It's the best kind of dad to be. That's why I know that eventually you're going to give Agent Rivers the keys to a boat so we can try to rescue my friend. I just don't know if you're going to do it soon enough to save him."

For a moment the room was silent except for the sound of the sergeant taking a deep breath while he considered what I'd said. His nostrils flared as he inhaled and he studied me for a moment before begrudgingly slapping a set of keys down onto the counter.

"If there's so much as a scratch . . ."

"There won't be," Marcus said as he snatched them up. "You're a good cop, Frank. And a good father. Thank you."

"Just do me a favor and find the kid," he said.

"That we will," Marcus said as he grabbed a pair of dingy orange life vests from a rack and handed them to us. "That we will."

We followed Marcus outside and had to hurry to keep up. "That was great work in there, Florian," he said, taking quick long strides. "Our boat's at the end of the dock."

I looked out at the water and felt a wave of uneasiness. "We're sure this is the best way to go, right?" I asked, hoping it sounded more like a question of strategy than a fear of barfing.

"Yes, for two reasons," he said. "First of all, it's our only chance to get close to the bridge without anyone noticing us."

This was the part he hadn't mentioned to the police officer—or anyone in the Bureau for that matter. We'd been taken off the case. A Child Abduction Rapid Deployment (CARD) team was in charge and they didn't want any help from us.

Our problem was that we were pretty sure they had it wrong.

"Secondly, they're going to put the bridge under surveillance and check all the roads and sidewalks leading to it," he said. "So they'll have everything fully covered up there. But I don't think they'll be checking the river traffic, and if you're right, that's where we need to be."

I gulped, realizing my theory had set this little adventure into motion, and wrestled my way into the life vest. The boat didn't have one of those clever names like *Oh, Say Can You Sea* or *When You Fish Upon a Star*. Instead, it was just called *MPDC-4*. But what it lacked in creativity, it made up for in stability. I was relieved by how solid it felt beneath my feet.

"You know, this isn't so bad," I said as I plopped down on a thickly padded seat. "It's actually kind of comfy."

"Too bad it's not ours." Marcus chuckled. "We're taking the *Zodiac*."

"The what-iac?"

"The *Zodiac*," he repeated. "It's the boat tied to the back of this one."

"You know," Margaret added as she pulled me back up by my life jacket and turned me toward a small inflatable tied to *MPDC-4*. "The teeny-tiny one."

Up until that point the only zodiac I knew was the collection of astrological signs like Capricorn and Aquarius. But apparently it was also the name of the world's most terrifyingly inadequate water vessel. My horoscope: rough seas ahead.

"Shouldn't we take one of the ones with, you know, sides?" (I was no longer concerned with sounding scared.)

"Remember the part about us trying not to attract attention?" Marcus said. "If the CARD team sees a boat with police markings invade their crime scene they'll go nuts. This one's completely unmarked. Besides, it's a whole lot faster."

"So you're telling me it's supersmall *and* superfast?" I said, trying to force a smile. "That's just . . ."

"Super?" joked Margaret.

I started to climb down into the *Zodiac*, but Marcus took me by the shoulders and stopped me. "You don't have to go, Florian. I mean it. You can stay right here and I'll have someone give you a ride home. In fact, it might be a good idea for both of you to stay. Even without the markings, there's a decent chance they'll spot us. And if they do there's no telling what kind of trouble there'll be for encroaching on someone else's case."

"No way," I answered. "A kid is missing. A kid I consider a friend. I'll go wherever the clues lead. Even if it means I have to take a submarine or ride in a helicopter."

"Me too," said Margaret. "Besides, if any one of us is getting in trouble, then all of us are."

He didn't say it but I could tell he was happy with our responses. We were in every way a team.

Once we were on board, Marcus untied the boat, maneuvered it out onto the river, and opened the throttle to full speed. As we raced toward the Key Bridge, the wind made it so my tie flapped in the air and kept slapping me in the face. I was too busy double clutching the safety rope that ran along our seat to do anything about it, so Margaret leaned over and tucked the tie into my life vest.

"You okay?" she asked, her voice barely audible over the whine of the engine.

I almost answered, but stopped when I realized that I wasn't sure if words or lunch would come out. Instead I just nodded and gripped the rope tighter.

"Look for anything suspicious," Marcus shouted so we could hear him.

"You mean more suspicious than the three of us?" Margaret responded.

There was so much mist spraying my face, I had to close my eyes as I tried to picture the crime scene in my head. A thirteen-year-old had disappeared despite being surrounded by dozens of people. There were no signs of foul play, no signs of anything out of the ordinary. The only clue we found was a sticky note with three words written in pen: "HELP KEY BRIDGE."

The boat slowed down and I opened my eyes to see the Francis Scott Key Bridge come into view. Spanning the Potomac between Washington and Rosslyn, Virginia, it looked much bigger from the river than it did from the land. Whenever we drove over it in our car, it just seemed like a road that happened to pass over water. There were no towers or cables holding it up. But from this vantage point, you could see the six massive arches supporting it.

Marcus continued to slow the engine until we were basically floating along with the current. He turned on his walkie-talkie and clicked through the channels until he heard some agents communicating up above.

"They're up there," he said. "Let's hope they won't notice us."

"What are we looking for?" asked Margaret.

"Anything suspicious," he replied. "On the water or along the riverside."

He nodded to the jogging-and-bike path that ran along the water.

We saw a couple of kayaks and a man riding a stand-up paddleboard, but none of them was suspicious. A pair of sightseeing cruisers approached. One was named the *General Washington* and the other the *President Jefferson*. Both were decorated with red, white, and blue banners, as well as a sign that advertised STAR-SPANGLED TOURS.

I scanned the decks of the first one but saw only tourists taking pictures. When it passed us, our boat started bobbing up and down in its wake and my stomach gurgled even more. I closed my eyes and tried not to give the second boat a show. (Imagine dozens of tourists snapping pictures as I puked over the edge of the *Zodiac*.) I focused all my mental energy on my stomach, trying to calm the storm inside me. Trying to ignore the motion and my sense of uselessness. Trying to block out everything.

And that's when I noticed the music playing over the speakers on the boat. My mind was so busy concentrating on my seasickness that my subconscious brain was free to identify that something was out of place.

I looked up at Marcus and Margaret and asked, "Why's a sightseeing boat in the capital of the United States and named after an American president playing the British national anthem?"

They both gave me a confused look.

"What are you talking about?" she asked.

I worried I might be hallucinating. "Don't you hear the song?"

They listened for a moment and Margaret began to sing along:

> *My country, 'tis of thee,*
> *Sweet land of liberty,*
> *Of thee I sing.*

"No, no, no," I said. "Those aren't the lyrics. The song is 'God Save the Queen.'" Having grown up in Europe, including three years spent in England, I was quite familiar with it. I started to sing the version that I knew:

God save our gracious Queen,
Long live our noble Queen,
God save the Queen.

Marcus smiled when he realized why I was confused. "I forgot that they both have the same tune," he said. "The Americans kept the music and wrote new lyrics to give it a completely different meaning."

I don't know if it was the dizziness, my stomach, the case, the clues, the music, or all of it. But in that moment I felt a surge moving up through my body. I couldn't tell if I was going to get sick, if my head was going to explode, or if I was going to solve the mystery right then and there. It just bubbled up through me. And then . . .

"I need to get off the boat," I said urgently.

"What's the matter?" asked Marcus. "Are you going to get sick?"

"No," I answered, my nausea instantly cured by my realization. "I told you I'd follow the clues wherever they lead, and they're not in the water."

"How do you know?" asked Margaret.

"It's complicated," I replied. "But the first thing you have to understand is that 'God Save the Queen' changes everything."

Molly Bigelow is NOT your average girl. She's one of an elite crew assigned the task of policing and protecting the zombie population of New York. *The Hunger Games* author Suzanne Collins says *Dead City* "breathes new life into the zombie genre."

EBOOK EDITIONS
ALSO AVAILABLE

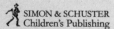

Visit the Whyville...

IN THE MIDDLE BOOK HIVE

Where you can:

- ◯ Discover great books!
- ◯ Meet new friends!
- ◯ Read exclusive sneak peeks and more!

Log on to visit now!
bookhive.whyville.net

FOLLOW THE CLUES.
CRACK THE CODE. STAY ALIVE.

When a mysterious cult begins to prey on London's apothecaries, the trail of murders grows closer and closer to Blackthorn's shop. With time running out, Christopher must use every skill he's learned to discover the key to a terrible secret with the power to tear the world apart.

"MAGIC, ADVENTURE, AND THINGS THAT GO BOOM—I LOVE THIS BOOK."
—EOIN COLFER, author of the bestselling Artemis Fowl series

THE BLACKTHORN KEY

KEVIN SANDS

EBOOK EDITION ALSO AVAILABLE

FROM
ALADDIN
SIMONANDSCHUSTER.COM/KIDS